The Marathon Photograph

'This may all seem strange to you, Andy, and I am a bit surprised myself, for until this moment I have not really considered how I felt when I found the body, never sorted out my reactions. So, to get on with it, I picked up the cube, which I am aware I should not have done, and holding it in my hand and turning it to try to determine what it was, I saw a glint of color from inside it, so I lifted it closer to look at it and saw what you saw just now. And having seen it, there was no question in my mind at all of dropping it back where I found it. I've never been more shaken in my life. I stood there, with the cold sweat breaking out on me, shaking like a leaf . . .'

'But, Neville, why?' I asked. 'I'll admit it is a clever thing, a beautiful piece of work, but . . .'

'You mean you didn't recognise it?'

'You mean the picture in the cube? Why should I?'

'Because it is a photograph of the Battle of Marathon.'

I gasped. 'A photograph? Marathon! How can you know? You are going dotty, Neville.'

Clifford D. Simak

THE
MARATHON
PHOTOGRAPH

A Methuen Paperback

A Methuen Paperback

THE MARATHON PHOTOGRAPH

British Library Cataloguing in Publication Data

Simak, Clifford D.
  The marathon photograph.
  I. Title
  813'.54[F]   PS3537.I54

  ISBN 0-413-59060-7

First world edition published 1986
by Severn House Publishers Ltd
This edition published 1987
by Methuen London Ltd
11 New Fetter Lane, London EC4P 4EE

The Introduction: Copyright © 1986 by Francis Lyall
The Birch Clump Cylinder:
From STELLAR 1, edited by Judy-Lynn del Rey.
Copyright © 1974 by Random House, Inc.
Reprinted by permission of Ballantine Books,
a division of Random House, Inc.
The Whistling Well:
Copyright © 1980 by Clifford D. Simak;
reprinted by permission of
the author and his agent, Kirby McCauley.
The Marathon Photograph:
Copyright © 1974 by Clifford D. Simak;
reprinted by permission of the author.
Grotto of the Dancing Deer:
Copyright © 1980 by The Conde Nast Publications, Inc;
reprinted by permission of the author.
First published in Analog Science Fiction/
Science Fact.

Printed and bound in Great Britain by
Richard Clay Ltd, Bungay, Suffolk

Introduction

In 1981, when in the United States on a research trip, I took a week-end out to go to Minneapolis where Clifford D Simak had agreed to meet me. I had begun to write a book about his fiction, his work being amongst my most favourite science fiction. Novels such as *City*, and *Way Station* had enthralled me in my teens and made 'Simak' a name to be watched for both in the magazines and amongst publishers' lists. A similar knowledge of his work may have brought you to pick up this book.

Meeting CDS was the high point of my 1981 trip. CDS was all that I had thought he might be from his books and stories. Thereafter, and regrettably for only a couple or so days, I explored the north-west corner of Grant County, Wisconsin, that triangular area bounded to the north and west by the Mississippi and the Wisconsin rivers, as the Wisconsin flows for its last few miles just north of the bluff country in which so much of CDS's fiction is set, and where he was born in August 1904. Seeing that country made me understand yet more of that gentle and good strength which comes through in his work. CDS is one who has managed to fuse science fiction with basic and ordinary human values in a way which few attempt, let alone succeed in carrying off. His childhood in Millville Township, Grant County, and his growing up among its country folk, imbibing their strengths and values, is a major part of the flavour of his work.

The best writers of all genres have an individuality which readily identifies their work. Plot, setting, character and subject, language and pace, all interact in a way which hall-marks their work. Clifford D Simak is one such. Over the years and by many high quality tales he has carved out a ledge (rather than a niche) within the pantheon of science fiction writers. Despite science fiction writing being only a part-time occupation until he retired from the newspaper world in 1976, his is a body of work of which many a full-time practitioner would be proud.

The art of the teller of tales runs back into the mists of time. Fundamentally, it is the art of entertainment. It may have begun as an ability given to some to take the attention of a grateful audience off the fears of the night and the privations of the morrow. Those huddling together for warmth and protection would have welcomed being carried elsewhere and into other emotions by the inventions of one of their number. Certainly the sense of wonder is present in the most ancient tales that have come down to us, and the best science fiction lies within that noble lineage.

No doubt some will disagree but, whatever the history of the matter, we need good stories. Some are fun, pure and simple. Others produce a frisson of fear. Yet others may be sombre and solemnising. On occasion, like the best of fairy stories, a tale may gently educate, but that is not its immediate aim. The curse of modern literature is the tract for the times, the self-indulgent puddle of diatribe poorly disguised as a story. Yet the really good story will have something in it which will linger in the mind, perhaps for years, and you will be glad that you read the story and stashed it away in that rag-bag of mental furniture everyone possesses. Such stories nourish the mind, and the emotions.

The sixty-thousand or so words of the stories here

collected show what I mean. They are fine examples of
the craft of the story-teller. An aspiring author can learn
much from them. Take *The Birch Clump Cylinder* and see
in its spare economy how to well-carpenter a tale. Every
sentence contributes by data or by atmosphere to the
impact. Each bit of information counts. In musical terms
it is a short quartet, stating, developing and concluding
its theme with clean lines. It contains an excellent
time-paradox, which is one of the most difficult types of
SF story to bring off nowadays. It has a new idea, that of
the time engine. It also has that delicate treatment of its
characters which we expect in a Simak tale, as Charley
Spencer, who begins the story somewhat discouraged
and battered by life, realises at the end that perhaps he
will go to the stars.

The Institute sited at Cramden Hall in *The Birch Clump
Cylinder* is the Coon Creek Institute, and that is another
give-away to those who know much of CDS's work. Coon
Creek and its variants appear in many Simak tales. It is
one of the many locations in his work whose origin can be
traced to an actual geographic spot. Coon Valley lies
some way north of the Wisconsin, and Highway 14/61
runs west down it from Viroqua and Westby through the
town of Coon Valley to La Crosse Southeast. It is a
glorious valley, with spreading side-valleys, and for his
purposes CDS has transposed it into Grant County,
Wisconsin. Other places in his stories require no such
moving. Wyalusing, Millville, Woodman and the like all
appear in CDS's stories, and can be compared with their
sources. Amongst the present collection I would draw
particular attention to two, *The Whistling Well*, and *The
Marathon Photograph*.

The Whistling Well feels authentic, despite the mystery
of its content. That authenticity comes from its being
firmly rooted in reality. We read of Thomas Parker's
search for the farm of his forebears, sited somewhere on

Parker's Ridge in bluff country, above a river. He is
directed to it from the town of Patch Grove, and is told
that it runs on from Military Ridge. There is a Patch
Grove in Grant County. It lies close to Highway 18,
some six miles south of the Bridgeport Bridge which
crosses the Wisconsin south of Prairie du Chien. I have
been there. To the north of Patch Grove and Highway 18
lies Military Ridge, which leads on to Sentinel Ridge,
and just to the north of a white dusty farm road on
Sentinel Ridge there is a well, which today clatters in the
wind, as it has done for years. That well was drilled by
CDS's grandfather, Ned Wiseman, who fought in the
Civil War, married Ellen Parker and won that farm from
the wild. You will see these and other connections in the
story itself. 'Thomas Parker' has close family connections
with his author. The setting, like the return of others to a
farm in other CDS's stories, is that of the scenes of CDS's
childhood and youth. The irises, the cottonwood trees,
the lilacs, the old timbered beams and the abandoned
hearthstones, the rosemary, the apple trees, and the
scrawny rose-bushes – the tender accuracy is that of love.

The same holds good for *The Marathon Photograph*. Life
in that bluff country is the mount for this jewel. Neville
wants to photograph some pink lady's slippers, and that
leads to everything. Those who know CDS's stories will
remember that Enoch Wallace knew where that rare-ish
plant grew on the land round his *Way Station*, the novel of
twenty years before this story was written. Platteville
limestone, laid down over the cylinder in this story, is
characteristic of the north-west corner of Grant County,
Platteville being a major town of the county, and a seat of
the University of Wisconsin. The real Kickapoo River,
which is also mentioned, enters the Wisconsin from the
north, across the river from the little town of Woodman,
and in this story we are told of the Lodge by reference to
the work of the local historian of Woodman County. We

are again reading of a story set in 'Simak country'. Many blind valleys in that region could shelter such a place as the Lodge, and the description of the countryside and the special touches, the lightning bugs and the squirrels, are those which only someone possessed of a deep knowledge and love of a place would incorporate.

But *The Marathon Photograph* is a more complex tale than its setting, and is one which repays several readings and returns to it. If *The Birch Clump Cylinder* is a quartet, this is a compressed symphony, which takes up many themes which CDS has treated elsewhere. There are many speculations gathered in it. There is the future of a blasted Earth, and those capable of travelling to the stars who are nonetheless scavenging amid their past. There is knowledge to be found, the knowledge of some vanished race from far across the galaxy, which has broadcast its knowledge as a last service before its extinction. What benefit will such alien knowledge be to our twisted posterity? There is the engimatic Stefan, said to be pyschopathic by his co-aevals. But who is the psychopath amongst them? Who is advanced; and what is advancement? There is the question of the time-chart and its powers. There is the question of the various photographs, Charlemagne, Marathon and . . ? And at the end of the story there is that pang about religion. It is a pang found in *The Whistling Well*, with its questions as to the religion of the dinosaurs, and it is found in several Simak novels which also speculate upon religion, faith and response. *Why Call Them Back From Heaven?*, *A Choice of Gods*, *Project Pope*, and *Special Deliverance* contain other musings on this theme, but none deliver quite the same bleakness as *The Marathon Photograph* does. Did Andrew Thornton successfully use the time saddle? And if so, what did he find? Read this one: put it aside for a week or so; then re-read it. Like much of the best music, it gives up its meaning gradually, and inexhaustibly.

The origin of the remaining story, *The Grotto of the Dancing Deer*, is different. It lies in CDS's non-fiction book *Prehistoric Man: The Story of Man's Rise to Civilisation* (1971), which itself sprang from his involvement for many years as the editor of a science series for the Minneapolis *Tribune*. One of the chapters is called *The World's First Paintings*. The cave paintings at Lascaux and other sites in the Pyrenees fascinated CDS, and he turned them over and over in his mind. The result is this story about the hidden grotto of paintings, and the way in which their discovery is arranged by someone who knows about them.

In *The Grotto of the Dancing Deer*, CDS displays all his qualities. There is mystery, and the ability to conjure up location. There is an intellectual puzzle. There is the deft evocation of character, and there is that profound sense that the old traditional values are best, and that they are worth preserving. Boyd could astonish the scientific community were he to reveal what he knows by the end of the story. But he will not. He has been trusted and will not prove himself unworthy of that trust. And in return his friend gives him another secret, but one which he can act on. Is there any wonder that this story won the Hugo, Nebula and Locus awards for 1980? If we persist with the musical comparisons, to me this story is kin to Barber's *Adagio for Strings*.

One last extraordinary fact, or, depending on how you count, two. All these stories have to do with time, and time stories are the most difficult of all science fiction to bring off. High standards have been set in the past, and there have been suggestions that it was no longer possible to write publishable time stories (as opposed to stories where time is simply a barrier to be gone through, the rest of the story taking place other-when). These four show that the opinion was wrong; but they also make it more difficult for future authors. It is extraordinary to find that this has been achieved by one of the Deans of science fiction producing these four stories in the fifth decade of his writing career. As you will see from the copyright credits, the earliest is a decade old. *The Grotto of the Dancing Deer* is the most recent, and was produced in CDS's seventy-fifth year, since when he has produced two excellent novels, with a third imminent. Extraordinary!

Aberdeen, Scotland   F Lyall
May, 1985

The Birch Clump Cylinder

As Bronson drove the car up the curving road that led to the front of Cramden Hall, I became aware that there had been some change, although it took a moment to figure what it was.

'The pagoda's gone,' I said.

'Blew down one night several years ago,' said Bronson. 'High wind came up. Flimsy thing, it was.'

Nothing else had changed, it seemed. Coon Creek didn't change. It stayed stodgy and a bit ramshackle and tried its humble best to seem of no account.

'Just as well it's gone,' said Bronson. 'It never seemed to fit. Just a little flighty for my taste.'

The car wheeled up and stopped in front of the pillared portico.

'You go on in,' said Bronson. 'Old Prather's waiting for you. I'll put away the car and bring in your bags.'

'Thanks for meeting me,' I said. 'It's been a long time, Bronson.'

'Fifteen years,' said Bronson. 'Maybe nearer twenty. None of us gets any younger. You never have been back.'

'No,' I said, 'I haven't.'

The car pulled away, and as it moved out of my line of vision I saw I had been wrong. For the pagoda wasn't gone; the pagoda was still there. It squatted in the evening light exactly as I remembered it, standing in the park-like area inside the driveway curve, with a pine at one corner of it and a sprawling yew along the side.

'Charles,' a voice said behind me. 'Charles, it's good to see you.'

I turned and saw it was Old Prather, fumbling down the steps towards me.

I went rapidly up to meet him, and we stood there for a moment, looking at one another in the fading light. He hadn't changed too much – a little older, perhaps, a bit more frazzled at the edges, but the same erect, stiff posture that barely escaped being military. The imagined scent of chalk dust still clung to him; he was as imperious as ever, but, I thought, looking at him, perhaps a shade more kindly mellowed with the years.

'The place looks the same as ever,' I said. 'Too bad the pagoda—'

'The pesky thing blew down,' he said. 'Gave us no end of trouble cleaning up the mess.'

We went trudging up the steps together. 'It was kind of you to come,' he said. 'As you may have gathered, we have a spot of trouble. On the phone, you understand, I couldn't be specific.'

'I jumped at the chance to come,' I said. 'Not doing anything, of course. Not since I was booted out of Time Research.'

'But that was two years ago. And you weren't booted.'

'It is three years,' I said, 'and I most emphatically was booted.'

'Dinner, I think, is ready,' he said, 'and we had best get to it. Old Emil—'

'Emil is still here?' I asked.

Old Prather chuckled thinly. 'We carry on,' he said. 'Bronson and myself and Emil. Young men coming up, but they are not quite ready. We all get crotchety and at times a little prickly. Emil, especially. He is crustier than ever and is apt to scold you if you're late for meals or don't eat quite enough. He takes it as a slur on his cooking.'

We reached the door and went into the foyer.

'And now,' I said, 'suppose you spell out this pagoda mummery.'

'You saw it, then?' he said.

'Of course I saw it. After Bronson had told me it had blown down. And it was still there when you said it had blown down. If this is some elaborate gag, just because I worked on Time Research—'

'It is no trick,' he said. 'It's part of the reason you are here. We'll talk about it later, but now we must go in to dinner or Emil will be outraged. Did I mention, by the way, that a couple of your classmates will be dining with us? Leonard Asbury. You remember him, of course.'

'Dr Prather,' I said, 'I have spent all these years trying not to remember him. He was a little twerp. And what other assorted alumni have you hauled in on this pagoda business?'

He said, without any shame at all, 'Only one other. Mary Holland.'

'She was the one who broke your heart. She went into music.'

'Charles,' he said, 'you mistake my function and the purpose of this institute if you think she broke my heart. The world could ill have afforded to lose the kind of music she has written.'

'So,' I said, 'a famous mathematician, a talented composer, a down-at-the-heels time researcher. When it comes to picking a team, you really go all out.'

His eyes took on a merry twinkle. 'Come on in to dinner,' he said, 'or Emil will wear out his tongue on us.'

2

The dinner had been a good one, simple and hearty — vichyssoise, a salad, prime ribs and a baked potato, with wine that was not bad at all.

Old Prather had done a lot of inconsequential and

rather pompous talking. The man was a good host; you have to give him that. The rest of us said little – the kind of tentative, exploratory talk that old acquaintances, too long separated, are likely to engage in.

I studied the two of them, and I knew that they were studying me as well. I could imagine both were wondering why Old Prather had invited me, for which I could not blame them.

Leonard Asbury, I decided, was still a little twerp. His thin black hair was slicked down against his skull. His face had a hard and foxy look. When he spoke, his thin lips scarcely moved. I didn't like the bastard a bit more than I ever did.

Mary was something else again. She had been a pretty girl, and we had had some dates – nothing serious, just dates. But now her beauty had settled into a sort of matronly composure, and I had the feeling there was a lot of emptiness behind that contented face.

It was damned unsettling – the two of them. I was uneasy and wished I had not come.

'And now,' said Old Prather, 'let us get down to business. For I suppose you must guess that there is some business. A rather urgent matter.'

He wiped his lips with his napkin, then bunched it on the table.

'I think,' he said, 'that Charles may have some inkling of it. He saw something when he came in that you others missed.'

Both Leonard and Mary looked at me. I didn't say a word. This was Old Prather's show; let him carry on.

'It seems quite likely,' he said, 'that we have a time machine.'

For a moment not one of us said anything, then Leonard leaned forward and asked, 'You mean someone here has invented—'

'I am sorry,' said Old Prather. 'I do not mean that at

all. A time machine has fallen into a clump of birch just above the little pond back of the machine shops.'

'Fallen?'

'Well, maybe not fallen. Appeared, perhaps, is a better word. Limpy, the gardener, found it. He is a simple lad. I guess none of you remember him. He came to us just a few years ago.'

'You mean to say it just showed up?' asked Mary.

'Yes, it just showed up. You can see it lying there, although not too clearly, for often it seems a little hazy. Objects at times appear around it, then disappear again – shunted in and out of time, we think. There have been some rather strange mirages around campus. The pagoda, for example.'

He said to me, 'The contraption seems to have a penchant for the pagoda.'

Leonard said, with barely concealed nastiness, 'Charles is our expert here. He is the time researcher.'

I didn't answer him, and for a long time nothing was said at all. The silence became a little awkward. Old Prather tried to cover up the awkwardness. 'You must know, of course,' he said, 'that each of you is here tonight for a special reason. Here is a situation that we must come to grips with and each of you, I'm sure, will make a contribution.

'But Dr Prather,' Mary said, 'I know less than nothing about the subject. I've never thought of time except in an abstract sense. I'm not even in the sciences. My whole life has been music. I've been concerned with little else.'

'That is exactly my point,' said Old Prather, 'the reason that you're here. We need an unsullied, an unprejudiced mind – a virgin mind, if you don't resent the phrase – to look at this phenomenon. We need the kind of thinking that can be employed by someone like yourself, who has never thought of time except, as you have said, in an abstract sense. Both Leonard and Charles have certain preconceptions on the subject.'

'I am gratified, of course,' said Mary, 'for the opportunity to be here, and quite naturally I am intrigued by what you call the "phenomenon". But actually, as you must realise, I have so provincial an attitude toward time that I doubt I can be any help at all.'

Sitting there and listening to her, I found myself in agreement with what she said. For once, Old Prather had managed to outsmart himself. His reason for bringing Mary in as a member of his team seemed utter nonsense to me.

'And I must tell you, as well,' said Leonard, 'that I have done no real work on time. Naturally, in mathematics – that is, in some areas of mathematics – time must be taken as a factor, and I am, of course, quite familiar with this. But I have never been primarily concerned with time, and I think you should know—'

Old Prather raised a hand to stop him. 'Not so fast,' he said. 'It seems to me that all of you are hurrying to disqualify yourselves.' He turned to me. 'So you are left,' he said. 'You've said exactly nothing.'

'Perhaps,' I said, 'because I have nothing to say.'

'The fact remains,' he insisted, 'that you were with Time Research. I'm burning with curiosity about the project. At least you can tell us something of what it's all about. I'm particularly interested in how you came to disassociate yourself.'

'I didn't disassociate myself. I was fired. I was booted out the door. You know the background of the project. The premise, and it is a solid premise, is that if we're ever to venture beyond the solar system – if we hope to reach the stars – we have to know a little more about the space-time concept than we know now.'

'I heard some rumor,' said Leonard, 'of a terrific row. My information said—'

'I don't know how terrific,' I said, 'but, as far as I was

concerned, it was sort of final. You see, I thought in terms of divorcing time from space, splitting the two into separate entities. And, goddam it, when you think of it, they are two separate factors. But science has talked so long of the space-time continuum that it has become an article of faith. There seems to be a prevalent idea that if you separate the two of them you tear the universe apart – that they are somehow welded together to make up the universe. But if you're going to work with time, you have to work with time alone, not with time and something else. Either you work with time or you work with nothing.'

'It all sounds highly philosophical to me,' said Old Prather.

'Here at Coon Creek,' I told him, 'you and several others taught us the philosophical approach. I remember what you used to tell us. Think hard and straight, you said, and to hell with all the curves.'

He coughed a highly artificial cough. 'I rather doubt,' he said, 'I phrased it quite that way.'

'Of course you didn't. Mine was an oversimplified translation. Your words were very much more genteel and greatly convoluted. And it's not as philosophical as it seems; it's just common sense – some of that hard, straight thinking you always urged upon us. If you are to work with anything, you must first know what you are working with, or at least have some theory as to what it is. Your theory can be wrong, of course.'

'And that,' said Leonard, 'was the reason you were canned.'

'That was the reason I was canned. An unrealistic approach, they said. No one would go along with it.'

While I had been talking, Old Prather had risen from the table and walked across the room to an ancient sideboard. He took a book from one of the drawers and walked back to the table. He handed the book to Leonard, then sat down again.

Leonard opened the book and started riffling through the pages. Suddenly he stopped riffling and stared intently at a page.

He looked up, puzzled. 'Where did you get this?' he asked.

'You remember I told you certain objects were appearing around the time machine,' said Old Prather. 'Appearing and then disappearing—'

'What kind of objects?' Mary asked.

'Different things. Mostly commonplace things. I recall there was a baseball bat. A battered bicycle wheel. Boxes, bottles, all kinds of junk. Close around the contraption. We let them go. We were afraid to come too close to it. One could get tangled up with the time effect. No one knows what it might do.'

'But someone,' said Leonard, 'managed to snag this book.'

'Limpy,' said Old Prather. 'He's a little short of sense. But, for some reason, he is intrigued by books. Not that he can do much reading in them. Especially in that one.'

'I should think not,' said Leonard. He saw that I was looking intently at him. 'All right, Charles,' he said, 'I'll tell you. It is mathematics. Apparently a new kind of mathematics. I'll have to study it.'

'From the future?' I asked.

'From about two centuries in the future,' said Old Prather, 'if you can believe the imprint date.'

'There is no reason, is there, to disbelieve it?'

'Not at all,' said Old Prather, happily.

'One thing,' I said, 'that you haven't mentioned. The dimensions of this machine of yours. What characteristics does it have?'

'If you're thinking of a container that was designed to carry a human passenger, it's not that at all. This one's not nearly big enough. It's cylindrical, three feet long or less. It's made of some sort of metal – a metal cylinder.

Grillwork of some sort at each end, but no sign of any operational machinery. It doesn't look like what one would think of as a time machine, but it does seem to have the effects of one. All the objects appearing and disappearing. And the mirages. We call them mirages for lack of a better term. The pagoda, for example, the pagoda that really did blow down, flicking on and off. People walking about, strangers who appear momentarily, then are gone. Occasional structures, like the ghosts of structures, not quite in the present, but not in the future, either. And they have to be from the future, for there's never been anything like them here. A boat on the pond. So far as I know, the pond has never had a boat. Too small for a boat. As you recall, just a little puddle.'

'You've taken precautions against someone stumbling into its field?'

'We've put a fence around it. Ordinarily, someone is watching to warn off stray visitors. But, as you know, we seldom have stray visitors. We'll all go out and have a look tomorrow, first thing after breakfast.'

'Why not now?' asked Leonard.

'No reason,' said Old Prather, 'but we wouldn't be able to see much. We have no lights out there. However, if you wish—'

Leonard made a gesture of agreement. 'Tomorrow's soon enough,' he said.

'Another thing you may have been wondering about,' said Old Prather, 'is how it got there. As I told you, the gardener found it. I said at first it fell, then corrected myself and said it had arrived. The correction was not quite an honest one. There is some evidence it fell – some broken branches in the birch clump that might have been broken when the thing plunged through the trees.'

'You say "fell,"' said Mary. 'Fell from where?'

'We are not sure, but we do have a hypothesis. Something happened west of here a few nights ago. A plane was reported down. Out in the hills. A wild and tangled country, as you may remember. Several people saw it falling. Searchers were sent out, but now the story is that there never was a plane. The news reports indicate it might have been a meteorite, mistaken for a plane. It is fairly clear that someone stepped in and quickly hushed it up. I made a few discreet inquiries of friends in Washington, and the word seems to be that a spaceship fell. Not one of our ships. All of ours can be accounted for. The supposition is that it may have been an alien ship.'

'And you think the time machine fell off the alien ship,' said Leonard. 'It was breaking up and—'

'But why would an alien ship carry a time machine?' asked Mary.

'Not a time machine,' I said. 'A time engine. A drive that uses time as a source of energy.'

3

Unable to sleep, I let myself out to go for a walk. The moon had just risen above the eastern hills, shedding a sickly light that barely dispersed the dark.

I hadn't been able to sleep. I had closed my eyes and tried, but then had been compelled to open them and stare up at the ceiling that was really not a ceiling, but just a square of darkness.

A time engine, I told myself. Time used as energy. Christ, then, I had been right! If it turned out that the thing in the clump of birch out there above the lake actually was an engine, then I had been right and all the others had been wrong. And, more than that, if time could be used as an energy, the universe lay open – not just the nearby stars, not just the galaxy, but the entire universe, everything that was. For if time could be manipulated – and to use it as a source of energy would mean that it would have to be capable of manipulation – then the distances of space would no longer count at all, would never need to be considered, and man could go anywhere he wished.

I looked up at the stars and I wanted to shout at them: Now your remoteness can no longer count with us. Your remoteness or the even more incredible remoteness of your sister stars that are so far that no matter how fiercely the fires may burn within them, we can catch no glimpse of them. Not even the dimmer stars, nor even the stars unseeable, are beyond our reach.

I wanted to yell at them, but of course I did not yell at, them. You do not yell at stars. A star is too impersonal a thing to think of yelling at.

I walked down the driveway and followed a sidewalk that angled up to the hill toward the observatory, and looking off to my left, I thought: Just over that little rise of ground in the clump of birch that stands above the pond. Trying to envision the cylinder that lay in the clump of birch, I wondered for the thousandth time if it might really be what I thought it was.

As I went around a curve in the winding walk, a man rose silently from a bench where he had been sitting. I stopped, somewhat startled by his sudden appearance; I had thought that at this time of night I would have been alone.

'Charley Spencer,' said the man. 'Can it be Charley Spencer?'

'It could be,' I said. His face was in the shadow, and I could not make it out.

'I must apologise,' he said, 'for intruding on your walk. I thought I was alone. You may not remember me. I am Kirby Winthrop.'

I went back through my memory, and a name came out of it. 'But I do remember you,' I said. 'You were a year or two behind me. I have often wondered what became of you.' Which was a lie, of course; I'd never thought of him.

'I stayed on,' he said. 'There's something about the place that gets into the blood. Doing some teaching. Mostly research. Old Prather pulled you in on the time machine?'

'Myself and some others,' I told him. 'What do you know about it?'

'Nothing, really. It's outside my field. I'm in cybernetics. That's why I'm out here. I often come out on the hill, when it's quiet, and think.'

'When it comes to cybernetics,' I told him, 'I rank as fairly stupid.'

'It's a wide field,' he said. 'I'm working on intelligence.'

'Indeed,' I said.

'Machine intelligence,' he said.

'Can machines be intelligent?' I asked.

He said, 'I rather think they can.'

'You're making progress, then?'

'I have a theory I am working on,' he said.

'Well, that is fine,' I said. 'I wish you all success.'

I sensed in him a hunger to talk, now that he had found someone new he could tell about his work; but I was not about to stand around with him out there in the night.

'I think I'll turn back,' I said. 'It's getting chilly and maybe now I can get some sleep.'

I turned to go, and he said to me, 'I'd like to ask you something, Charley. How many people have you ever told you got your education at Coon Creek?'

The question startled me, and I turned back to face him.

'That's a funny question, Kirby.'

'Maybe so,' he said, 'but how many have you?'

'As few as possible,' I said. I hesitated for a moment,

waiting for him to speak, and when he didn't, I said, 'It was good to see you, Kirby,' and I headed back toward the hall.

But he called after me, and I swung around again.

'There is something else,' he said. 'What do you know of the history of Coon Creek?'

'Not a thing,' I said. 'I'm not even curious.'

'I was,' he said, 'and I did some checking. Do you know there has never been a cent of public money in this place? And in all its history, it has never had a research grant. So far as I can find, it has never applied for one.'

'There is an endowment of some sort,' I said. 'Someone by the name of Cramden, way back in the eighties. Cramden Hall is named for him.'

'That is right,' said Winthrop, 'but there never was a Cramden. Someone put up the money in his name, but there never was a Cramden. No one by the name of Cramden.'

'Who was it, then?'

'I don't know,' he said.

'Well,' I said, 'I don't suppose it makes a great deal of difference now. Coon Creek is here and that is all that counts.'

I started off down the walk again, and this time he let me go.

Good to see you, I had told him, but it had not been good. I scarcely remembered the man – a name out of the past, a name without a face. And I still did not have the face, for his back had been toward the moon and I had not seen his face.

And all that silly talk about did I often mention Coon Creek and who had endowed the college. What had the man been getting at and why should he be so concerned? In any case, I told myself, it did not matter to me. I wasn't going to be here long enough for it to matter to me.

I went back to the driveway. When I got to the foot of
the stairs that led to Cramden Hall, I turned around and
looked back down the curving drive toward the man-
icured landscape that lay within the curve.

Coon Creek, I thought. God, yes, Coon Creek. It was a
place you never mentioned because it had a corny sound
and people always asked you where it was and what kind
of school it was; and there really were no answers. 'I
never heard of it,' they'd say, 'but it sounds so interesting.'

You couldn't tell them they had never heard of it
because they were not supposed to hear of it, that it was
quietly tucked away and had its corny name so that no
one in his right mind would ever want to go to it. Nor
could you tell them that the school selected its students
rather than the students selecting it, that it went out and
recruited brains, exactly as other colleges, intent on
winning football teams, recruited brawn.

'Brains' would not be the precise word, since some of
us – and I was one of them – were not all that brainy.
Rather it was an ability of a certain kind which had never
been quite defined, an approach to problems and a
philosophy that was undefined as well, known, of course,
to certain people, but certainly not to those chosen ones
who were invited to become students at Coon Creek.
How they found us no one really knew, and who was
behind it all was unknown as well. The government, I
had always thought, but I had been far from sure. The
selection process had a sort of undercover secret
sneakiness that had the feel of government. Although, if
what Winthrop had told me was correct, it was not
government.

Not all of us, of course, turned out as well as might have
been expected. I had not for one. And Mary . . . well,
maybe Mary hadn't either. During her days at the institute, I recalled, she had exhibited an interest in

economics that must have been upsetting to Old Prather and perhaps to many others; and then she had gone off at a tangent into music, which must have been the farthest from what those who engineered the college must have had in mind. Leonard, of course, was another case – one of the more successful ones – a brilliant mathematician who was pushing science beyond logic and into an intuitional area that gave some promise of arriving at some understanding not only of the mechanism, but of the purpose of the universe.

I stood for a short time looking at the driveway and the area it enclosed – waiting, I think, for the pagoda to come back again; but it did not come back, so I turned and went up the stairs.

4

The time machine, as Old Prather had described it, was wedged between the boles of the clump of birch. It had a sort of hazy, flickering look to it, but not so much that it could not be seen with some clarity. The space around it was fairly clear of time-debris. There were a tennis ball and an old boot, but that was all. While we watched the boot went away.

'We did a little preliminary investigation,' Old Prather said, 'before the three of you arrived. We rigged up a camera on a boom and got it in as close as we could manage to photograph the entire surface – all, that is, except the portion of it that is resting on the ground. We lost the first camera. It was shifted into time or whatever happens when you get too close to it. We didn't lose the second camera, and we found out one thing. Close down against the ground and shielded by a tree trunk is what appears to be a control of some sort.'

Old Prather opened the folder he carried underneath his arm, and we crowded around to look. A couple of photographs showed what seemed to be a control, a circular patch set into the metal of the cylinder – but that was all, a circular patch. There were no calibration marks, but there seemed to be three litle projections set into the edge of the circle. The projections at one time could have been tied into a control mechanism of some sort, but there was nothing to indicate they had.

'Nothing else?' asked Leonard.

'Only a couple of rough spots on the surface,' said Old Prather. He found the photographs. 'One on one end, another on the opposite end.'

'They could mark the positions,' I said, 'where the time engine was mounted on the craft. If it is a time engine and was on a craft. The spots where the engine broke from its mountings.'

'You're fairly certain of that, though,' said Leonard, a little nastily.

'It's an idea,' I said. 'That is all it is.'

'It seems to me,' said Leonard, 'that we need more people in on this than just the three of us. Charley here is the only one of us who knows anything about time and—'

'Whatever I know of it,' I told him, 'is only theoretical. I'd have no idea how a contraption like this could be put together. We can't just go wading in. If it is a time engine, I would guess it is only idling; but we still have no idea what a time-force can do. Maybe it's not too powerful, but the power is probably fluctuating. If we start messing around with it and do something that turns it on full power—'

Old Prather nodded gravely. 'I can realise the danger,' he said 'but if it's possible to do so, I'd prefer to see this discovery kept within the family. It would be against my grain to share it with someone else – especially with the government. And if we went to anyone it should be the government.'

'Our time machine would be easier to work with,' said

Mary, 'if we could get it out of that birch clump – out into the open where we could roll it around and get at it better.'

'We had thought of that,' said Old Prather, 'but we were afraid to touch it. We could pry it out of there, of course, but—'

'I don't think,' said Leonard, 'that we should touch it yet. Even the slightest jar might affect the mechanism. Trouble is we're working in the dark. We don't know what we have. If we could turn it off – but I haven't the faintest idea how to turn it off. That control circle, maybe, if it is a control. But how do you get to it to turn it?'

'You said Limpy got the book,' Mary said to Old Prather. 'How did he manage it? Did he reach in and get it?'

'He was carrying a hoe,' Old Prather said. 'He hooked it out with that.'

'Maybe,' said Leonard, 'someone in the shops could rig up something we could use to manipulate the circle. Attach it to a long handle, and we might reach in. There are those three little nibs on the outside of the circle. If we had a tool of some sort that would engage them, we might be in business.'

'That's fine,' I said, 'but would you know which way to turn the circle?'

We needn't have worried which way to turn it. The shop rigged up a tool, working from the photographs. The first time it was not quite the right size. The second time around it fit, but it didn't work. It slid past the nibs. The metal had what appeared to be an oily quality. There seemed no way to get a grip on it. The shop went on, working into the night, trying to engineer something that might do the job. But all of us, even the shop, knew there was little chance.

That night at dinner we tried to talk it out. There was

no talking it out, however. The problem had too many angles to it – not just how we'd get the engine shut down, but what we'd do with it once it was shut down. How did you go about investigating a time mechanism? If you were lucky, of course, you might take it apart, photographing and diagramming each step in taking it apart. You might even be able to take it apart and put it back together and still not be able to find what made it operate. Even when you had it all spread out, even when you had examined every component of it, understanding the relationship of each component to all the rest of it, the principle might still escape you.

Chances were, we agreed, that stripping it down would involve some danger, perhaps considerable danger. Somewhere within that metal cylinder was a factor no one understood. Checks and balances were built into the machine to control that factor. Unbalance this system and you would be face to face with time, or that factor we called 'time'; and no one, absolutely no one, knew what time might be.

'What we'll need,' said Leonard, 'is something that will contain time, that will insulate it.'

'Okay,' I said. 'That is exactly it. Something that damps the time factor while we work, so that we aren't blown back into the Carboniferous or forward to the point where the universe is approaching heat death.'

'I don't think the time force is that strong,' Old Prather objected.

'Probably not, the way it is now,' said Leonard. 'Charley thinks the engine is idling, maybe barely functioning. But if that thing out there is what we think it is, it has to have the requisite power to drive a spaceship over many light-years.'

'The damping factor would have to be something that is immaterial,' I said. 'Something that is not a part of the material universe. Anything that has mass would be affected by time. What we need is something upon which time has no effect.'

'Light, maybe,' said Mary. 'Lasers—'

Leonard shook his head. 'Either time affects light,' he said, 'or light has established its own time parameter. It travels only so fast. And while it may not seem so, it is actually material. Light can be bent by a strong magnetic field. What we need is something outside time and independent of it.'

'Well, maybe the mind, then,' said Mary. 'Thought. Telepathic thought aimed at the engine, establishing some sort of rapport with it.'

'That fits our specifications,' Old Prather agreed, 'but we're a thousand years too soon. We don't know what thought is. We don't know how the mind operates. We have no telepaths.'

'Well,' said Mary, 'I did my best. I came up with two bad ideas. How about the rest of you?'

'Witchery,' I said. 'Let us go to Africa or the Caribbean and get us a good witch doctor.'

I had meant to be facetious, but it didn't seem to strike them that way. They sat there looking at me like three solemn owls.

'A resonance of some sort,' said Leonard.

'I know about that,' said Mary, 'and it wouldn't work. You're talking about a kind of music, and I know music. Time is a part of music. Music is based on time.'

Leonard frowned. 'I said it wrong,' he told us, 'and without too much thought. What I was thinking about were atoms. Perhaps there is no such thing as time in atomic structure. Some investigators have advanced the theory. If we could line up atoms, get them into some sort of random step—' He shook his head. 'No, it wouldn't work. There's no way in God's world that it could be done, and even if it could, I guess it wouldn't work.'

'A strong magnetic field,' said Old Prather. 'Wrap the engine in a magnetic field.'

'Fine,' I said. 'That might do the trick. The field might bend and contain time. But, aside from the fact that we can't build such a field . . .'

'If we could,' said Mary, 'we couldn't work inside the field. What we're talking about is how to control time so we can investigate the engine.'

'The only thing left is death, I said. 'Death is a timeless thing.'

'Can you tell me what death is?' snapped Leonard.

'No, I can't,' I said, grinning at him.

'You're a smart aleck,' he said viciously. 'You always were.'

'Now, now,' said Old Prather, completely horrified. 'Let us have more wine. There's still some left in the bottle.'

'We aren't getting anywhere,' said Mary, 'so what difference does it make? Death sounds as good to me as any of the others.'

I bowed to her with mock gravity, and she made a face at me. Old Prather went skipping around the table like a concerned cricket, pouring the wine.

'I hope,' he said, 'the boys in the shop can come up with something that will turn the control dial.'

'If they don't,' said Mary, 'we'll do it by hand. Have you ever thought how the human hand is often more versatile than the finest tool?'

'Trouble is,' said Leonard, 'that however ingenious the tool may be, it is going to be awkward. You have to stand so far away, and you're working at a dirty angle.'

'But we can't do it by hand,' Old Prather protested. 'There is the time effect.'

'On little things,' said Mary. 'On books and tennis balls and boots. Never on a living thing. Never on anything with the mass of a human body.'

'I still wouldn't want to try it,' said Leonard.

5

We tried it. We had to try it.

The tools the shop dreamed up wouldn't work, and we simply couldn't leave the time machine there in the clump of birch. It was still operating. While we watched, a battered wrist watch, a tattered notebook, an old felt hat appeared and disappeared. And momentarily the boat was upon the pond that had never known a boat.

'I spent last night with the mathematics text,' said Leonard, 'hoping I might find something that might help us, but I didn't find a thing. Some new and intriguing concepts, of couse, but nothing that could be applied to time.'

'We could construct a good strong fence around it,' said Old Prather, 'and leave it there until we know what to do with it.'

'Nonsense,' said Mary. 'Why, for heaven's sake, a fence? All we need to do is step in there—'

'No,' said Leonard. 'No, I don't think we should. We don't know—'

'We know,' said Mary, 'that it can move small objects. Nothing of any mass at all. And all of them are inanimate. Not a single living thing. Not a rabbit, not a squirrel. Not even a mouse.'

'Maybe there aren't any mice,' said Old Prather.

'Fiddlesticks,' said Mary. 'There are always mice.'

'The pagoda,' said Leonard. 'Quite some distance from this place and a rather massive structure.'

'But inanimate,' said Mary.

'You mentioned mirages, I believe,' I said to Old Prather. 'Buildings and people.'

'Yes,' he said, 'but merely shadows. Very shadowy.'

'God. I don't know,' I said. 'Maybe Mary's right. Maybe it has no real effect on anything that's living.'

'We'd be gambling, you know,' said Leonard.

'Leonard, that is what is wrong with you,' said Mary. 'I've been wondering all this time what was wrong with you. And now it seems I know. You never gamble, do you?'

'Never,' said Leonard. 'There is no sense in gambling. It's a sucker's game.'

'Of course not, said Mary. 'A computer for a brain. A lot of little mathematical equations to spell out life for you. You're different from the rest of us. I gamble; Charley, here, would gamble—'

'All right,' I said, 'cut out the arguing. I'll do the job. You say fingers are better than tools, so let us find out. All you have to tell me is which way I should turn it.'

Mary grabbed my arm. 'No, you don't,' she said. 'I was the one who started this. I'm the one to do it.'

'Why don't the two of you,' Leonard said in his nasty, twerpy way, 'draw straws to determine which one of you it'll be?'

'Now that is a good idea,' Mary said. 'But not the two of us. It'll be the three of us.'

Old Prather had been doing some twittering around, and now he blurted out, 'I think this is the height of foolishness. Drawing straws, indeed! I do not approve of it. I approve it not at all. But if straws are being drawn, there must be four of them.'

'Not on your life,' I said. 'If it should happen that the three of us are caught up in time and whisked very swiftly hence, someone must be left to explain it all. And you are the man to do that. You explain everything so well. You've been doing it for years.'

It was insane, of course. If we had taken all of thirty seconds to really talk it over, we would not have done it. But each of us had got caught up in the excitement and each of us had invested some ego in the project, and we couldn't back away. Leonard could have, probably, but he'd got caught up in a sort of stubborn pride. If he had said, 'No, I won't go along with it,' that might have ended it. But if he'd done that he'd have confessed to cowardliness, and he couldn't quite do that.

We didn't draw straws. We put three pieces of paper in Old Prather's hat, the pieces of paper marked, one, two, and three.

Mary got the one, Leonard the two, and I came up with three.

'Well, that settles it, said Mary. 'I'm the first to try it. Which is only right, since I suggested it.'

'The hell with that,' I said. 'Just tell me which way it should be turned – if it can be turned, that is.'

'Charles,' said Mary, primly, 'after all these years you are being chauvinistic, and you know very well I'll insist upon my right.'

'Oh, for Christ sake,' said Leonard, 'let her go ahead! She's the one who's sure.'

'I still do not approve,' said Old Prather, rather fussily, 'but you did draw numbers. I wash my hands of the matter. I disassociate myself from it.'

'Bully for you,' I said.

'I shall turn it clockwise,' said Mary. 'After all, that is the way—'

'You can't be sure,' said Leonard. 'Just because that is a human convention—'

Before I could reach out to stop her, she darted into the clump of birch and was bending over to reach the control circle. Fascinated, I watched in that split second when her fingers gripped and turned. I distinctly saw the control circle move. So she had been right, after all, I thought: fingers were better than a tool.

But even as I thought it, Mary disappeared, and around the cylinder there was a sudden flurry of many different articles dredged out of time and moved into the present from the past and future and – once arrived – shunted to the past or future, continuing the direction of their flow. There was a pocket radio, a brightly colored shirt, a knapsack, a couple of children's blocks, a pair of spectacles, a woman's purse and, so help me God, a rabbit.

'She turned it the wrong way!' I shouted. 'It's no longer idling.'

Leonard took a quick step forward, then paused, took another slow step. For an instant more I waited, and when he didn't move, I reached out an arm and swept him to one side. Then I was in the clump of birch and reaching down. I felt my fingers on the circle, felt the flesh sink into the little nibs, and my brain roared at me: counterclockwise, counterclockwise, counterclockwise . . .

I don't really remember turning the control circle, but suddenly the time debris that had been washing over and around my feet was no longer there, and neither was the cylinder.

Slowly I straightened up and backed out of the clump of birch. 'What the hell happened to the engine?' I asked. And as I said it, I turned around to catch the response of the others, but there were no others.

I stood alone and shivered. Everything was the way it had been before. The day was still a sunny day, the birch clump looked the same as ever, and the pond was the same as well, although not quite the same, for now a small rowboat was pulled up on the shore.

I shivered at the sight of it, then held myself stiff and straight to forestall further shivering. My mind clicked over reluctantly and told me what I fought against believing.

Had I done the job? I wondered. Had I turned the engine off, or had Leonard had to go in and complete the job? Then I knew I must have done it, for neither Leonard nor Old Prather would have followed up.

The cylinder was gone and gone how long ago? I

wondered. And where was Mary? And what about the boat?

I headed across the slope toward Cramden Hall, and as I went along I kept a sharp outlook for changes. But if there were changes, they were not pronounced enough for me to notice them. I remembered that through the years Coon Creek did not change. It stayed stodgy and a bit ramshackle and tried its humble best to seem of no account. It wore an ancient coat of protective coloration.

There were a few students about. As I came down to the sidewalk that led to the curving driveway, I met one face to face; but he paid no attention to me. He was carrying a clutch of books underneath his arm and seemed in something of a hurry.

I climbed the stairs in front of the hall and let myself into the hushed twilight of the foyer. There was no one around, although I heard the sound of footsteps going down a hall that was out of sight.

Standing there, I felt unaccountably an outsider, as if I had no right to be there. Just down the hall was Old Prather's office. He would have the answer, and whether I belonged or not, I told myself, I was entitled to the answer.

But there was a chilliness in the place that I didn't like, a chilliness and, now that the sound of distant footsteps had ceased, a silence that went with the chilliness.

I half turned to leave, then turned back, and as I turned, a man came out of the door of Old Prather's office. He headed down the hall toward me, and I stayed standing there, not knowing what to do, not wanting to turn about and leave, wishing in a frantic moment that the man coming down the hall should fail to see me there, although I knew that undoubtedly he had seen me.

It was time displacement, I knew, a sense of time displacement. It was something we had often talked about in idle moments back at Time Research. If a man were moved in time, would he feel out of place? Would he sense a different time frame? Was man aware of time? Was a specific temporal bracket an unseen factor of personal environment?

The light in the hall was dim, and the face of the man who was approaching me was a very ordinary face – a stereotype, one of those faces that one sees on thousands of different people, with so little remarkable about them that there is nothing to remember, with the end result that all of these faces come to look alike.

The man slowed his pace as he came nearer to me. Then he said, 'Is there any way I can help you? Are you looking for someone?'

'Prather,' I said.

A change came over his face, a sudden change that was at once fear and wonderment. He stopped and stared at me.

'Charley?' he asked, questioningly. 'You are Charley Spencer?'

'That is who I am,' I said. 'And now about Old Prather.'

'Old Prather's dead,' he said.

'And you?'

'You should remember me. I am Kirby Winthrop. I took over Prather's place.'

'Fast work,' I said. 'I saw you just the other night.'

'Fifteen years ago, said Kirby. 'Our meeting on Observatory Hill was fifteen years ago.'

It staggered me a little, but I guess I was prepared for it. I hadn't really thought about it; I had not allowed myself to think about it. If I had any real reaction, it would have been relief that it was not a hundred years.

'What about Mary?' I asked. 'Has she shown up yet?'

'I think perhaps you could stand a drink,' said Kirby. 'I know damn well I could. Let's go and have a drink.'

He came up to me and linked his arm in mine, and we went marching down the hall to the room he'd left.

He said to the girl in the outer office, 'Hold all calls. I'm in to no one.' Then he hustled me into the inner office.

He almost pushed me into a deep, upholstered chair in one corner of the office and went to a small bar under the windows.

'Have you a preference, Charley?'

'If you have some scotch,' I said.

He came back with the glasses, handed one to me and sat down in an opposite chair.

'Now we can talk,' he said. 'But get down a slug of liquor first. You know, all these years I've been sort of expecting you. Not wondering when you would show up, of course, but if you would.'

'Afraid I would,' I said.

'Well, maybe something of that, too. But not very much. Slightly embarrassing, of course, but—'

Kirby left the sentence hanging in the air. I took a snort of scotch. 'I asked you about Mary.'

He shook his head. 'She won't be coming. She went the other way.'

'You mean into the past.'

'That's right. We'll talk about it later.'

'I see the time contraption's gone. Did I shut it off?'

'You shut it off.'

'I wondered if maybe Leonard or Old Prather—'

He shrugged. 'Not Leonard. He was a basket case. And Old Prather – well, you see, Old Prather never was a part of it. He never really was a part of anything at all. He stood outside of everything. Only an observer. That was his way of life, his function. He had people doing things for him—'

'I see,' I said. 'So you got it out of there. Where is it now?'

'It? You mean the engine?'

'That's right.'

'Right at the moment it's up in the Astrophysics Building.'

'I don't remember—'

'It's new,' he said. 'The first new building on the campus for more than fifty years. It and the spaceport.'

I came half out of my chair, then settled back again. 'A spaceport—'

'Charley,' said Kirby, 'we've been out to the Centauri system and 61 Cygni.'

'We?'

'Us. Right here. Coon Creek Institute.'

'Then it worked!'

'You're damned right it worked.'

'The stars,' I said. 'My God, we're going to the stars! You know, that night when we met out on the hill . . . that night I wanted to shout to the stars, to tell them we were coming. What have you found out there?'

'Centauri, nothing. Just the three stars. Interesting, of course, but no planets. Not even space-debris. A planetary system never formed, never got started. Cygni has planets, twelve of them, but nothing one could land on. Methane giants, others that are in the process of forming crusts, one burned-out cinder close up to the sun.'

'Then there are planets.'

'Yes, millions, billions of solar systems. Or at least that's what we think.'

'You say us. How about the others? How about the government?'

'Charley,' he said, 'you don't understand. We are the only ones who have it. No one else.'

'But—'

'I know. They've tried. We've said no. Remember, we are a private institution. Not a dime of federal or state or any other kind of money—'

'Coon Creek,' I said, half choking at the ridiculous thought of it. 'Good old Coon Creek, come into its own.'

'We've had to set up a security system' Kirby said primly. 'We have all sort of sensors and detectors and guards three deep around the place. It plays hell with the budget.'

'You say you have the engine here. That means you were able to build others.'

'No problem. We took the engine apart. We charted it, we measured its components, we photographed it. We have it down on tape to the last millimeter of it. We can build hundreds of them, but there is one thing—'

'Yes?'

'We don't know what makes it work. We missed the principle.'

'Leonard?'

'Leonard's dead. Has been for years. Committed suicide. I don't think even if he'd lived—'

'There's something else,' I said. 'You wouldn't have dared to tinker with the engine if you hadn't had a way to damp the time effect. Old Prather and the three of us kicked that one around—'

'Intelligence,' said Kirby.

'What do you mean – intelligence?'

'You remember that night we talked. I told you I was building—'

'An intelligent machine!' I shouted. 'You mean to tell me?'

'Yes, I mean to tell you. An intelligent machine. I almost had it that night I talked with you.'

'Mary was on the right track, then,' I said. 'That night at dinner she said "thought". Telepathic thought aimed at the engine. You see, it had to be some immaterial thing. We beat our brains out and could come up with nothing. But we knew we had to have a damper.'

I sat silently, trying to get it all straight in my mind.

'The government suspects,' I said, 'where you got the engine. There was that crashed spaceship.'

'There was a spaceship,' said Kirby. 'They finally got enough of it to guess how it was built. Picked up some organic matter, too, but not enough to get a good idea of its passengers. They suspect, of course, that we got the engine, although they aren't even sure there was an engine. We've never admitted we found anything at all. Our story is we invented it.'

'They must have known, even from the first, something funny was going on,' I pointed out. 'Mary and I disappeared. That would have taken some explanation. Not myself, of course, but Mary was something of a celebrity.'

'I'm a bit ashamed to tell you this,' said Kirby, and he did look a bit ashamed. 'We didn't actually say so, but we made it seem that the two of you had run off together.'

'Mary wouldn't have thanked you for that,' I told him.

'After all,' he said, defensively, 'the two of you had some dates while you were students.'

'There's one thing you've not been telling me,' I said. 'You said Mary went into the past. How do you know that?'

He didn't answer for a while, and then he finally asked a question. 'You remember that night we talked out on the hill?'

I nodded. 'We talked about your intelligent machine.'

'More than that. I told you there never was a man named Cramden, that the endowment money came from someone else but was credited to a non-existent Cramden.'

'So what does that have to do with it?'

'It was something that Old Prather remembered. He told me about the argument you had about the drawing of the straws or paper slips out of a hat or something of the sort. Leonard wanted none of it. Shutting off the engine the way you did it, he said, was a gamble. And Mary said sure it was a gamble and that she was willing to gamble.'

He stopped and looked at me. I shook my head. 'I don't get it,' I said. 'Is all this supposed to have some meaning?'

'Well, it turned out later that she was a gambler – a most accomplished gambler. She'd racked up half a fortune in the stock market. No one knew too much about it until later. She did it rather quietly.'

'Wait a second, there,' I said. 'She was interested in economics. She took some courses and did a lot of reading. Economics and music. I've always wondered why she was ever chosen for the institute—'

'Precisely,' he said. 'Many times, in the dead of night, I've wondered that myself, and each time I have been somewhat frightened at how it all turned out. Can you imagine the sort of killing that someone like Mary, with her kind of background, could make if they were thrown a hundred years into the past? They'd know the pattern. They'd know what to buy, when to get in, when to get out. Not specifically, of course, but from their knowledge of history.'

'Are you just guessing or do you have some facts?'

'Some facts,' he said. 'Not too many. A few. Enough for an educated guess.'

'So little Mary Holland is thrown into the past, makes herself a bundle, endows Coon Creek Institute—'

'More than that,' he said. 'There was the initial endowment, of course, the one that got us started. And then, about fifteen years ago, about the time the time-engine business started, there was a supplementary endowment that had been in escrow in a New York bank for years, pegged to be paid off at a given time. A rather handsome sum. This time there was a name – a certain

Genevieve Lansing. From the little I could find she had been an eccentric old character who was an accomplished pianist, although she never played in public. And the thing that made her so eccentric was that at a time when no one else ever even thought about it, she was utterly convinced that some day man would go out to the stars.

I said nothing for a long time and neither did he. He got up and brought a bottle from the bar and splashed some more liquor in our glasses.

Finally I stirred in my chair. 'She knew,' I said. 'She knew you'd need that supplementary endowment to develop a spaceship and spaceport facilities.'

'That's what we used it for,' he said. 'We named the ship the *Genevieve Lansing*. I ached to call it the *Mary Holland*, but I didn't dare.'

I finished off my liquor and put the glass down on a table. 'I wonder, Kirby,' I said, 'if you'd put me up for a day or two. Until I can get my feet under me. I don't quite feel up to walking out immediately.'

'We couldn't let you go in any case,' said Kirby. 'We can't have you turning up. Remember, you and Mary Holland ran off together fifteen years ago.'

'But I can't just stay here. I'll take a different name if you think I should. At this late date, no one would recognise me.'

'Charley,' he said, 'you wouldn't just be staying here. There's work for you to do. You may be the one man alive who can do the job that's waiting.'

'I can't imagine . . .'

'I told you we can build time engines. We can use them to go out to the stars. But we don't know why they work. We don't know the principle. That's an intolerable situation. The job's less than half done, there's still a lot to do.'

I got out of the chair slowly. 'Coon Creek,' I said. 'Tied forever to Coon Creek.'

He held out his hand to me. 'Charley,' he said, 'we're glad to have you home.'

And standing there, shaking hands with him, I reminded myself it need not be Coon Creek forever. One of these days I might be going to the stars.

The Whistling Well

He walked the ridge, so high against the sky, so windswept, so clean, so open, so far-seeing. As if the very land itself, the soil, the stone, were reaching up, standing on tiptoe, to lift itself, stretching toward the sky. So high that one, looking down, could see the backs of hawks that swung in steady hunting circles above the river valley.

The highness was not all. There was, as well, the sense of ancientness and the smell of time. And the intimacy, as if this great high ridge might be transferring to him its personality. A personality, he admitted to himself, for which he had a liking, a thing that he could wrap, as a cloak, around himself.

And through it all, he heard the creaking of the rocker as it went back and forth, with the hunched and shriveled, but still energetic, old lady crouched upon it, rocking back and forth, so small, so dried up, so emaciated that she seemed to have shrunken into the very structure of the chair, her feet dangling, not reaching the floor. Like a child in a great-grandfather chair. Her feet not touching, not even reaching out a toe to make the rocker go. And, yet, the rocker kept on rocking, never stopping. How the hell, Thomas Parker asked himself, had she made the rocker go?

He had reached the ultimate point of the ridge where steep, high limestone cliffs plunged down toward the river. Cliffs that swung east and from this point continued along the river valley, a stony rampart that fenced in the ridge against the deepness of the valley.

He turned and looked back along the ridge and there, a mile or so away, stood the spidery structure of the windmill, the great wheel facing west, toward him, its blades a whir of silver movement in the light of the setting sun.

The windmill, he knew, was clattering and clanking, but from this distance, he could hear no sound of it, for the strong wind blowing from the west so filled his ears that he could pick up no sound but the blowing of the wind. The wind whipped at his loose jacket and made his pants' legs ripple and he could feel its steady pressure at his back.

And, yet, within his mind, if not within his ears, he still could hear the creaking of the rocker, moving back and forth within that room where a bygone gentility warred against the brusqueness of present time. The fireplace was built of rosy brick, with white paneling placed around the brick, the mantel loaded with old figurines, with framed photographs from another time, with an ornate, squatty clock that chimed each quarter hour. There had been furniture of solid oak, a threadbare carpet on the floor. The drapes at the large bow windows, with deep window seats, were of some heavy material, faded over the years to a nondeterminate coloring. Paintings with heavy gilt frames hung on the walls, but the gloom within the room was so deep that there was no way of seeing what they were.

The woman-of-all-work, the companion, the housekeeper, the practical nurse, the cook, brought in the tea, with bread-and-butter sandwiches piled on one plate and delicate cakes ranged on another. She had set the tray on the table in front of the rocking old lady and then had gone away, back into the dark and mysterious depths of the ancient house.

The old lady spoke in her brittle voice, 'Thomas,' she said, 'if you will pour. Two lumps for me, no cream.'

Awkwardly, he had risen from the horsehair chair. Awkwardly he had poured. He had never poured before. There was a feeling that he should do it charmingly and delicately and with a certain genteel flair, but he did not have the flair. He had nothing that this house or this old lady had. His was another world.

He had been summoned here, imperatively summoned, in a crisp little note on paper that had a faint scent of lavender, the script of the writing more bold than he would have expected, the letters a flowing dignity in old copperplate.

I shall expect you, she had written, *on the afternoon of the 17th. We have matters to discuss.*

A summons from the past and from seven hundred miles away and he had responded, driving his beaten-up, weather-stained, lumbering camper through the flaming hills of a New England autumn.

The wind still tugged and pushed at him, the windmill blades still a swirl of movement and below him, above the river, the small, dark shape of the circling hawk. Autumn then, he told himself, and here another autumn, with the trees of the river valley, the trees of other far-off vistas, taking on the color of the season.

The ridge itself was bare of trees, except for a few that still clustered around the sites of homesteads, the homesteads now gone, burned down or weathered away or fallen with the passage of the years. In time long past, there might have been trees, but more than a hundred years ago, if there had been any, they had fallen to the ax to clear the land for fields. The fields were still here, but no longer fields; they had known no plow for decades.

He stood at the end of the ridge and looked back across it, seeing all the miles he had tramped that day, ex-

ploring it, getting to know it, although why he felt he
should get to know it, he did not understand. But there
was some sort of strange compulsion within him that,
until this moment, he had not even questioned.

Ancestors of his had trod this land, had lived on it and
slept on it, had procreated on it, had known it as he, in a
few short days, would never know it. Had known it and
had left. Fleeing from some undefinable thing. And that
was wrong, he told himself, that was very wrong. The
information he'd been given had been somehow garbled.
There was nothing here to flee from. Rather, there was
something here to live for, to stay for – the closeness to
the sky, the cleansing action of the wind, the feeling of
intimacy with the soil, the stone, the air, the storm, the
very sky itself.

Here his ancestors had walked the land, the last of
many who had walked it. For millions of years unknown,
perhaps unsuspected, creatures had walked along this
ridge. The land was unchanging, geologically ancient, a
sentinel of land standing as a milepost amidst other lands
that had been forever changing. No great .mountain-
building surges had distorted it, no glacial action had
ground it down, no intercontinental seas had crept over
it. For hundreds of millions of years, it had been a
freestanding land. It had stayed as it was through all that
time, with only the slow and subtle changes brought
about by weathering.

He had sat in that room from out of the past and
across the table from him had been the rocking woman,
rocking even as she drank the tea and nibbled at the
bread-and-butter sandwich.

'Thomas,' she had said, speaking in her old brittle
voice, 'I have a job for you to do. It's a job that you must
do, that only you can do. It's something that's important
to me.'

Important to her. Not to someone else, to no one else

but her. It made no difference to whom else it might be important or unimportant. To her, it was important and that was all that counted.

He said, amused at her, at her rocking and her intensity, the amusement struggling up through the out-of-placeness of the room, the woman and the house, 'Yes, Auntie, what kind of job? If it's one that I can do . . .'

'You can do it,' she said, tartly. 'Thomas, don't get cute with me. It's something you can do. I want you to write a history of our family, of our branch of the Parkers. I am aware there are many Parkers in the world, but it's our direct line in which my interest lies. You can ignore all collateral branches.'

He had stuttered at the thought. 'But, Auntie, that would take a long time. It might take years.'

'I'll pay you for your time,' she'd said. 'You write books about other things. Why not about the family? You've just finished a book about paleontology. You spent three years or more on that. You've written books on archaeology, on the old Egyptians, on the ancient trade routes of the world. Even a book on old folklore and superstitions and, if you don't mind my saying so, that was the silliest book I ever read. Popular science, you call it, but it takes a lot of work. You talk to many different people, you dig into dusty records. You could do as much for me.'

'But there'd be no market for such a book. No one would be interested.'

'I would be interested,' she said sharply, the brittle voice cracking. 'And who said anything about publication? I simply want to know. I want to know, Thomas, where we came from and who we are and what kind of folks we are. I'll pay you for the job. I'll insist on paying you. I'll pay you . . .'

And she named a sum that quite took his breath away. He had never dreamed she had that kind of money.

'And expenses,' she said. 'You must keep a very close accounting of everything you spend.'

He tried to be gentle with her, for quite obviously she was mad. 'But, Auntie, you can get it at a much cheaper figure. There are genealogy people who make a business of tracing back old family histories.'

She sniffed at him. 'I've had them do the tracing. I'll give you what I have. That should make it easier for you.'

'But if you have that—'

'I suspect what they have told me. The record is unclear. To my mind, it is. They try too hard to give you something for your money. They set out to please you. They gild the lily, Thomas. They tell about the manor house in Shropshire, but I'm not sure there ever was a manor house. It sounds just a bit too pat. I want to know if there ever was or not. There was a merchant in London. He dealt in cutlery, they say. That's not enough for me, I must know more of him. Even in our New England, the record is a fuzzy one. Another thing, Thomas. There are no horse thieves mentioned. There are no gallows birds. If there are horse thieves and gallows birds, I want to know of them.'

'But, why, Auntie? Why go to all the bother? If it is written, it will never be published. No one but you and I will know. I hand you the manuscript and that is all that happens.'

'Thomas,' she had said, 'I am a mad old woman, a senile old woman, with only a few years left of madness and senility. I should hate to have to beg you.'

'You will not have to beg me,' he had said. 'My feet, my brain, my typewriter are for hire. But I don't understand.'

'Don't try to understand,' she'd told him. 'I've had my way my entire life. Let me continue to.'

And, now, it had finally come to this. The long trail of

the Parkers had finally come down to this high and
windswept ridge with its clattering windmill and the
little clumps of trees that had stood around the
farmsteads that were no longer there, to the fields that
had long been fallow fields, to the little spring beside
which he had parked the camper.

He stood there above the cliffs and looked down the
slope to where a tangled mass of boulders, some of them
barn-size or better, clustered on the hillside, with a few
clumps of paper birch growing among them.

Strange, he thought. These were the only trees, other
than the homestead trees, that grew upon the ridge, and
the only boulder clump. Not, certainly, the residue of
glaciation, for the many Ice Age glaciers that had come
down across the Middle West had stopped north of here.
This country, for many miles around, was known as the
driftless area, a magic little pocket that, for some reason
not yet known, had been bypassed by the glaciers while
they crunched far south on each side of it.

Perhaps, at one time, he told himself, there had been
an extrusive rock formation jutting from the ridge, now
reduced by weathering to the boulder cluster.

Idly, with no reason to do so, without really intending
to, he went down the slope to the cluster with its growth
of paper birch.

Close up, the boulders were fully as large as they had
appeared from the top of the ridge. Lying among the half
dozen or so larger ones were many others, broken
fragments that had been chipped off by frost or running
water, perhaps aided by the spalling effect of sunlight.

Thomas grinned to himself as he climbed among
them, working his way through the cracks and intervals
that separated them. A great place for kids to play, he
thought. A castle, a fort, a mountain to childish imagination. Blowing dust and fallen leaves through the
centuries had found refuge among them and had formed

a soil in which were rooted many plants, including an array of wild asters and goldenrod, now coming into bloom.

He found, towards the center of the cluster, a cave or what amounted to a cave. Two of the larger boulders, tipped together, formed a roofed tunnel that ran for a dozen feet or more, six feet wide, the sides of the boulders sloping inward to meet some eight feet above the tunnel's floor. In the center of the tunnel lay a heaped pile of stones. Some kid, perhaps, Thomas told himself, had gathered them many years ago and had hidden them here as an imagined treasure trove.

Walking forward, he stooped, and picked up a fistful of the stones. As his fingers touched them, he knew there was something wrong. These were not ordinary stones. They felt polished and sleek beneath his fingertips, with an oily texture to them.

A year or more ago, in a museum somewhere in the west – perhaps Colarado, although he could not be sure – he had first seen and handled other stones like these.

'Gastroliths,' the grey-bearded curator had told him. 'Gizzard stones. We think they came from the stomachs of herbivorous dinosaurs – perhaps all dinosaurs. We can't be certain.'

'Like the grit you find in a chicken's craw?' Thomas had asked.

'Exactly,' the curator said. 'Chickens pick up and swallow tiny stones, grains of sand, bits of shell to help in the digestion of their food. They simply swallow their food. They have no way to chew it. The grit in the gizzard does the chewing for them. There's a good possibility, one might even say, a high possibility, the dinosaurs did the same, ingesting pebbles to do the chewing for them. During their lifetime, they carried these stones, which become highly polished, and then when they died—'

'But the greasiness? The oily feeling?'

The curator shook his head. 'We don't know. Dinosaur oil? Oil picked up from being so long in the body?'

'Hasn't anyone tried to extract it? To find out if there is really oil?'

'I don't believe anyone has,' the curator said.

And here, in this tunnel, in this cave, whatever one might call it, a pile of gizzard stones.

Squatting, Thomas picked them over, gathering a half dozen of the larger ones, the size of small hen's eggs, or less, feeling the short hairs on his neck tingling with an ancient, atavistic fear that should have been too far in the distant past to have been felt at all.

Here, millions of years ago, perhaps a hundred million years ago, a sick, or injured, dinosaur had crept in to die. Since that time, the flesh was gone, the bones turned into dust, but remaining was the pile of pebbles the long-gone dinosaur had carried in its gizzard.

Clutching the stones in his hand, Thomas settled back on his heels and tried to re-create, within his mind, what had happened here. Here the creature had lain, crouched and quivering, forcing itself, for protection, as deeply into this rock-grit hole as had been possible. It had snorted in its sickness, whimpered with its pain. And it had died here, in this same spot he now occupied. Later had come the little scavenging mammals, tearing at its flesh . . .

This was not dinosaur land, he thought, not the kind of place the fossil hunters came to hunt the significant debris of the past. There had been dinosaurs here, of course, but there had not been the violent geological processes which would have resulted in the burying and preservation of their bones. Although, if there had been, they'd still be here, for this was ancient land, untouched by the grinding glaciers that must have destroyed, or deeply buried, so many fossil caches.

But here, in this cluster of shattered boulders, he had

stumbled on the dying place of a thing that no longer walked on earth. He tried to imagine what form that now extinct creature might have taken, what it would have looked like when it still had life within it. But there was no way that he could know. There had been so many different shapes of them, some of them known by their fossils, perhaps many still unknown.

He fed the selected gizzard stones into the pocket of his jacket and when he crawled from the tunnel and walked out of the pile of boulders, the sun was bisected by the jagged hills far to the west. The wind had fallen with the coming of the evening hours and he walked in a hushed peace along the ridge. Ahead of him, the windmill clattered with subdued tone, clanking as the wheel went slowly round and round.

Short of the windmill, he went down the slope to the head of a deep ravine that plunged down toward the river. Here, beside the spring, parked beneath a massive cottonwood, his camper shone whitely in the creeping dusk. Well before he reached it, he could hear the sound of water gushing from the hillside. In the woods farther down the slope, he could hear the sound of birds settling for the coming night.

He rekindled the campfire and cooked his supper and later sat beside the fire, knowing that now it was time to leave. His job was finished. He had traced out the long line of Parkers to this final place, where shortly after the Civil War, Ned Parker had come to carve out a farm.

In Shropshire there had been, indeed, a manor house. And he had found, as well, that the London merchant had not dealt in cutlery, but in wool. There had been no horse thieves, no gallows birds, no traitors, no real scamps of any kind. The Parkers had been, in fact, a plodding sort of people, not given to greatness, nor to evil. They had existed nonspectacularly, as honest yeomen, honest merchants, farming their small acres, managing their small businesses. And finally crossing the water to New England, not as pioneers, but as settlers. A few of them had fought in the Revolutionary War, but were not distinguished warriors. Others had fought in the Civil War, but had been undistinguished there, as well.

There had, of course, been a few notable, but not spectacular, exceptions. There had been Molly Parker, who had been sentenced to the ducking stool because she talked too freely about certain neighbors. There had been Jonathon, who had been sentenced to the colonies because he had the bad judgement of having fallen into debt. There had been a certain Teddy Parker, a churchman of some sort (the evidence was not entirely clear), who had fought a prolonged and bitter battle in the court with a parishioner over pasture rights held by the church which had been brought into question.

But these were minor matters. They scarcely caused a ripple on the placidity of the Parker tribe.

It was time to leave, he told himself. He had tracked the family, or this one branch of the family, down to this high ridge. He had found the old homestead, the house burned many years ago, now marked only by the cellar excavation, half filled with the litter of many years. He had seen the windmill and had stood beside the whistling well, which had not whistled for him.

Time to leave, but he did not want to leave. He felt a strange reluctance at stirring from this place. As if there were more to come, more that might be learned – although he knew there wasn't.

Was this reluctance because he had fallen in love with this high and windy hill, finding in it some of the undefinable charm that must have been felt by his great-great-grandfather? He had the feeling of being trapped and chained, of having found the one place he was meant to be. He had, he admitted to himself, the sense of belonging, drawn and bound by ancestral roots.

That was ridiculous, he told himself. By no matter what weird biochemistry within his body he had come to think so, he could have no real attachment to this place. He'd give himself another day or two and then he'd leave. He'd make that much concession to this feeling of attachment. Perhaps, by the end of another day or two, he'd have enough of it, the enchantment fallen from him.

He pushed the fire more closely together, heaped more wood upon it. The flames caught and flared up. He leaned back in his camp chair and stared out into the darkness, beyond the firelit circle. Out in the dark were darker humps, waiting, watching shapes, but they were, he knew, no more than clumps of bushes – a small plum tree or a patch of hazel. A glow in the eastern sky forecast a rising moon. A quickening breeze, risen after the sunset calm, rattled the leaves of the big cottonwood that stood above the camp.

He scrooched around to sit sidewise in the chair and when he did, the gizzard stones in his jacket pocket caught against the chair arm and pressed hard against his hip.

Reaching a hand into his pocket, he took them out. Flat upon his palm, he held them out so the firelight fell upon them. He rubbed a thumb against them. They had the feel and look of velvet. They glistened in the dancing firelight. The gloss on them was higher than was ever found in the polished pebbles that turned up in river gravel. Turning them, he saw that all the depressions, all the concave surfaces, were as highly polished as the rest of the stone.

The stones found in the river gravel had obtained their polish by sand action, swirling or washed along the riverbed. The gizzard stones had been polished by being rubbed together by the tough contracting muscles of a gizzard. Perhaps some sand in the gizzard, as well, he thought, for in jerking up a plant from sandy soil, the dinosaur would not be too finicky. It would ingest the sand, the clinging bits of soil, along with the plant. For years, these stones had been subjected to continuous polishing action.

Slowly, he kept turning the stones with a thumb and finger of the other hand, fascinated by them. Suddenly, one of them flashed in the firelight. He turned it back and it flashed again. There was, he saw, some sort of an irregularity on its surface.

He dropped the other two into his pocket and leaned forward toward the fire with the one that had flashed lying in his palm. Turning it so that the firelight fell full upon it, he bent his head close above it, trying to puzzle out what might be there. It looked like a line of writing, but in characters he had never seen before. And that had to be wrong, of course, for at the time the dinosaur swallowed the stone, there had been no such thing as writing. Unless someone, later on, within the last century or so – he shook his head in puzzlement. That made no sense, either.

With the stone clutched in his hand, he went into the camper, rummaged in a desk drawer until he found a small magnifying glass. He lit a gas lantern and turned it up, placed it on the desk top. Pulling over a chair, he sat down, held the stone in the lantern light, and peered at it through the glass.

If not writing, there was something there, engraved into the stone – the engraving worn as smooth and sleek as all the rest of it. It was no recent work. There was no possibility, he told himself, that the line that resembled engraving could be due to natural causes. He tried to make out exactly what it was, but in the flicker of the lantern, it was difficult to do so. There seemed to be two triangles, apex pointing down in one, up in the other and the two of them connected midpoint by a squiggly line.

But that was as much as he could make of it. The

engraving, if that was what it was, was so fine, so delicate, that it was hard to see the details, even with the glass. Perhaps a higher-power glass might show more, but this was the only magnifier he had.

He laid the stone and glass on the desk top and went outside. As he came down the steps, he felt the differentness. There had been blacker shapes out in the darkness and he had recognised them as clumps of hazel of small trees. But now the shapes were bigger and were moving.

He stopped at the foot of the steps and tried to make them out, to pinpoint the moving shapes, but his eyes failed to delineate the shapes, although at times they seemed to catch the movement.

You're insane, he told himself. There is nothing out there. A cow or steer, perhaps. He had been told, he remembered, that the present owners of the land, at times, ran cattle on it, pasturing them through the summer, penning them for finishing in the fall. But in his walks about the ridge, he'd not seen any cattle and if there were cattle out there, he thought that he would know it. If cattle moved about, there should be a crackling of their hocks, snuffling as they nosed at grass or leaves.

He went to the chair and sat down solidly in it. He reached for a stick and pushed the fire together, then settled back. He was too old a hand at camping, he assured himself, to allow himself to imagine things out in the dark. Yet, somehow, he had got the wind up.

Nothing moved beyond the reaches of the firelight and still, despite all his arguments with himself, he could feel them out there, sense them with a sense he had not known before, had never used before. What unsuspected abilities and capacities, he wondered, might lie within the human mind?

Great dark shapes that moved sluggishly, that hitched

along by inches, always out of actual sight, but still circling in close to the edge of light, just beyond its reach.

He sat rigid in the chair, feeling his body tightening up, his nerves stretching to the tension of a violin string. Sitting there and listening for the sound that never came, for the movement that could only be sensed, not seen.

They were out there, said this strange sense he had never known before, while his mind, his logical mind, cried out against it. There is no evidence, said his human mind. There need be no evidence, said this other part of him; we know.

They kept moving in. They were piling up, for there were a lot of them. They were deadly silent and deliberate in the way they moved. If he threw a chunk of wood out into the darkness, the chunk of wood would hit them.

He did not throw the wood.

He sat, unmoving, in the chair. I'll wear them out, he told himself. If they are really out there, I will wear them out. This is my fire, this is my ground. I have a right to be here.

He tried to analyse himself. Was he frightened? He wasn't sure. Perhaps not gibbering frightened, but probably frightened otherwise. And, despite what he said, did he have the right to be here? He had a right to build the fire, for it had been mankind, only mankind, who had made use of fire. None of the others did. But the land might be another thing; the land might not be his. There might be a long-term mortgage on it from another time.

The fire died down and the moon came up over the ridgetop. It was almost full, but its light was feeble-ghostly. The light showed nothing out beyond the campfire, although, watching closely, it seemed to Thomas that he could see massive movement farther down the slope, among the trees.

The wind had risen and from far off, he heard the faint

clatter of the windmill. He craned his head to try to see the windmill, but the moonlight was too pale to see it.

By degrees, he relaxed. He asked himself, in something approaching fuzzy wonder, what the hell had happened? He was not a man given to great imagination. He did not conjure ghosts. That something incomprehensible had taken place, there could be little doubt – but his interpretation of it? That was the catch; he had made no interpretation. He had held fast to his life-long position as observer.

He went into the camper and found the bottle of whiskey and brought it out to the fire, not bothering with a glass. He sat sprawled in the chair, holding the bottle with one hand, resting the bottom of it on his gut. The bottom of the bottle was a small circle of coldness against his gut.

Sitting there, he remembered the old black man he had talked with one afternoon, deep in Alabama, sitting on the ramshackle porch of the neat, ramshackle house, with the shade of a chinaberry tree shielding them from the heat of the late-afternoon sun. The old man sat easily in his chair, every now and then twirling the cane he held, its point against the porch floor, holding it easily by the shaft, twirling it every now and then, so that the crook of it went round and round.

'If you're going to write your book the way it should be written,' the old black man had said, 'you got to look deeper than the Devil. I don't suppose I should be saying this, but since you promise you will not use my name . . .'

'I won't use your name,' Thomas had told him.

'I was a preacher for years,' the old man said. 'And in those years, I learned plenty of the Devil. I held him up in scorn; I threatened people with him. I said, "If you don't behave yourselves, Old Devil, he will drag you down them long, long stairs, hauling you by your heels, with your head bumping on the steps, while you scream and plead and cry. But Old Devil, he won't pay no attention to your screaming and your pleading. He won't even hear you. He'll just haul you down those stairs and cast you in the pit." The Devil, he was something those people could understand. They'd heard of him for years. They knew what he looked like and the kind of manners that he had. . .'

'Did it ever help?' Thomas had asked. 'Threatening them with the Devil, I mean.'

'I can't be sure. I think sometimes it did. Not always, but sometimes. It was worth the try.'

'But you tell me I must go beyond the Devil.'

'You white folks don't know. You don't feel it in your bones. You're too far from the jungle. My people, we know. Or some of us do. We're only a few lifetimes out of Africa.'

'You mean . . .'

'I mean you must go way back. Back beyond the time when there were any men at all. Back to the older eons. The Devil is a Christian evil – a gentle evil, if you will, a watered-down version of real evil, a shadow of what there was and maybe is. He came to us by way of Babylon and Egypt and even the Babylonians and Egyptians had forgotten, or had never known, what evil really was. I tell you the Devil isn't a patch on the idea he is based on. Only a faint glimmer of the evil that was sensed by early men – not seen, but sensed, in those days when men chipped the first flint tools, while he fumbled with the idea of the use of fire.'

'You're saying that there was an evil before man? That figures of evil are not man's imagining?'

The old man grinned, a bit lopsidely, at him, with still a serious grin. 'Why should man,' he asked, 'take to himself the sole responsibility for the concept of evil?'

He'd spent, Thomas remembered, a pleasant afternoon on the porch, in the shade of the chinaberry tree, talking with the old man and drinking elderberry wine. And, at other times and in other places, he had talked with other men and from what they'd told him had been able to write a short and not too convincing chapter on the proposition that a primal evil may have been the basis for all the evil figures mankind had conjured up. The book had sold well, still was selling. It had been worth all the work he had put into it. And the best part of it was that he had escaped scot-free. He did not believe in the Devil or any of the rest of it. Although, reading his book, a lot of other people did.

The fire burned down, the bottle was appreciably less full than when he'd started on it. The landscape lay mellow in the faint moonlight. Tomorrow, he told himself, I'll spend tomorrow here, then I'll be off again. Aunt's Elsie's job is finished.

He got up from the chair and went in to bed. Just before he went to bed, it seemed to him that he could hear, again, the creaking and the scuffing of Auntie's rocking chair.

After breakfast, he climbed the ridge again to the site of the Parker homestead. He'd walked past it on his first quick tour of the ridge, only pausing long enough to identify it.

A massive maple tree stood at one corner of the cellar hole. Inside the hole, raspberry bushes had taken root. Squatting on the edge of the hole, he used a stick he had picked up to pry into the loam. Just beneath the surface lay flakes of charcoal, adding a blackness to the soil.

He found a bed of rosemary. Picking a few of the leaves, he crushed them in his fingers, releasing the sharp smell of mint. To the east of the cellar hole, a half dozen apple trees still survived, scraggly, branches broken by the winds, but still bearing small fruit. He picked one of the apples and when he bit into it, he sensed a taste out of another time, a flavor not to be found in an apple presently marketed. He found a still flourishing patch of rhubarb, a few scrawny rosebushes with red hips waiting for the winter birds, a patch of iris so crowded that corms had been pushed above the surface of the ground.

Standing besides the patch of iris, he looked around. Here, at one time, more than a century ago, his ancestor had built a homestead – a house, a barn, a chicken house, a stable, a granary, a corncrib, and perhaps other buildings, had settled down as a farmer, a soldier returned from the wars, had lived here for a term of years and then had left. Not only he but all the others who had lived on this ridge as well.

On this, his last trip to complete the charge that had been put upon him by that stange old lady hunched in her rocking chair, he had stopped at the little town of Patch Grove to ask his way. A couple of farmers sitting on a bench outside a barbershop had looked at him – reticent, disbelieving, perhaps somewhat uneasy.

'Parker's Ridge?' they'd asked. 'You want to know the way to Parker's Ridge?'

'I have business there,' he'd told them.

'There ain't no one to do business with on Parker's Ridge,' they'd told him. 'No one ever goes there.'

But when he'd insisted, they'd finally told him. 'There's only one ridge, really,' they'd said, 'but it's divided into two parts. You go north of town until you reach a cemetery. Just short of the cemetery, you take a left. That puts you on Military Ridge. You keep to the high ground. There are some roads turning off, but you stay on top the ridge.'

'But that you say is Military Ridge. What I want is Parker's Ridge.'

'One and the same,' said one of the men. 'When you reach the end of it, that's Parker's Ridge. It stands high above the river. Ask along the way.'

So he'd gone north of town and taken a left before he reached the cemetery. The ridge road was a secondary route, a farm road, either unpaved or paved so long ago and so long neglected that it bore little trace of paving. Small farms were strung along it, little ridgetop farms, groups of falling-down buildings surrounded by scant and runty fields. Farm dogs raced out to bark at him as he passed the farms.

Five miles down the road a man was taking mail out of a mailbox. Thomas pulled up. 'I'm looking for Parker's Ridge,' he said. 'Am I getting close?'

The man stuffed the three of four letters he'd taken from the box into the rear pocket of his overalls. He stepped down to the road and stood beside the car. He was a large man, rawboned. His face was creased and wrinkled and wore a week of beard.

'You're almost there,' he said. 'Another three miles or so. But would you tell me, stranger, why do you want to go there?'

'Just to look around,' said Thomas.

The man shook his head. 'Nothing there to look at. No one there. Used to be people there. Half a dozen farms. People living on them, working the farms. But that was long ago. Sixty years – no, maybe more than that. Now they all are gone. Someone owns the land, but I don't know who. Someone runs cattle here. Goes out West in the spring to buy them, runs them on pasture until fall, then rounds them up and feeds them grain, finishing them for the market.'

'You're sure there's no one there?'

'No one there now. Used to be. Buildings, too. Houses and old farm buildings. Not any longer. Some of them burned. Kids, most likely, setting a match to them. Kids probably thought they were doing right. The ridge has a bad reputation.'

'What do you mean, a bad reputation? How come a bad–'

'There's a whistling well, for one thing. Although I don't know what the well has to do with it.'

'I don't understand. I've never heard of a whistling well.'

The man laughed. 'That was old Ned Parker's well. He was one of the first settlers out there on the ridge. Come home from the Civil War and bought land out there. Got it cheap. Civil War veterans could buy government land at a dollar an acre and, at that time, this was all government land. Ned could have bought rich, level land out on Blake's Prairie, some twenty miles or so from here, for the same dollar an acre. But not him. He knew what he wanted. He wanted a place where timber would be handy, where there'd be a running spring for water, where he'd be close to hunting and fishing.'

'I take it the place didn't work out too well.'

'Worked out all right except for the water. There was one big spring he counted on, but a few dry years came along and the spring began running dry. It never did run dry, but Ned was afraid it would. It is still running. But Ned, he wasn't going to be caught without water, so, by God, he drilled a well. Right on top that ridge. Got in a well driller and put him to work. Hit a little water, but not much. Went deeper and deeper and still not enough. Until the well driller said, "Ned, the only way to get water is to go down to the river level. But the rest of the way it is going to cost you a dollar and a quarter a foot." Now, in those days, a dollar and a quarter was a lot of money, but Ned had so much money sunk in the well already that he said to go ahead. So the well driller went ahead. Deepest well anyone had ever heard of. People used to come and just stand there, watching the well being drilled. My grandfather told me this, having heard it from his father. When the hole reached river level, they did find water, a lot of water. A well that would never run dry. But pumping was a problem. That water had to be pumped straight up a long way. So Ned bought the biggest, heaviest, strongest windmill that was made and that windmill set him back a lot of cash. But Ned never complained. He wanted water and now he had it. The windmill never gave no trouble, like a lot of windmills did. It was built to last. It's still there and still running, although it's not pumping water anymore. The pump shaft broke years ago. So did the vane control, the lever to shut off the wheel. Now that mill runs all the time. There's no way to shut it off. Running without grease, it's gotten noiser and noiser. Some day, of course, it will stop, just break down.'

'You told me a whistling well. You told me everything else, but nothing about a whistling well.'

'Now that's a funny thing,' the farmer said. 'At times, the well whistled. Standing on the platform, over the bore, you can feel a rush of wind. Then the rush gets strong enough, it is said to make a whistling sound. People say it still does, although I couldn't say. Some people used to say it only whistled when the wind was from the north, but I can't swear to that, either. You know how people are. They always have answers for everything whether they know anything about it or not. I understand that those who said it only whistled when the wind was from the north explained it by saying that a strong north wind would blow directly against the cliffs facing the river. There are caves and crevices in those cliffs and they said some of the crevices ran back into the ridge and that the well cut through some of them. So a north wind would blow straight back along the crevices until it hit the well and the come rushing up the bore.'

'It sounds a bit far-fetched to me,' said Thomas.

The farmer scratched his head. 'Well, I don't know. I can't tell you. It's only what the old-time people said. And they're all gone now. Left their places many years ago. Just pulled up and left.'

'All at once?'

'Can't tell you that either. I don't think so. Not all in a bunch. First one family and then another, until they all were gone. That happened long ago. No one would remember now. No one knows why they left. There are strange stories – not stories, really, just things you hear. I don't know what went on. No one killed, so far as I know. No one hurt. Just strange things. I tell you, young man, unless I had urgent business there, I wouldn't venture out on Parker's Ridge. Neither would any of my neighbors. None of us could give you reasons, but we wouldn't go.'

'I'll be careful,' Thomas promised.

Although, as it turned out, there'd been no reason to be careful. Rather, once he'd reached the ridge, he'd felt that inexplicable sense of belonging, of being in a place where he was supposed to be. Walking the ridge, he'd felt this barren backbone of land had transferred, or was in the process of transferring, its personality to him and he'd taken it and made it fit him like a cloak, wrapping himself in it, asking himself: Can a land have a personality?

The road, once Military Ridge had ended beyond the last farmhouse and Parker's Ridge began, had dwindled to a track, only a grassy hint that a road once had existed there. Far down the ridge he had sighted the windmill, a spidery construction reared against the sky, its wheel clanking in the breeze. He had driven on past it and then had stopped the camper, walking down the slope until he had located the still-flowing spring at the head of the ravine. Going back to the camper, he had driven it off the track and down the sloping hillside, to park it beneath the cottonwood that stood above the spring. That had been the day before yesterday and he had one more day left before he had to leave.

Standing now, beside the iris bed, he looked around

him and tried to imagine the kind of place this may have
been – to see it with the eyes of his old ancestor, home
from the wars and settled on acres of his own. There
would still have been deer, for this old man had wanted
hunting, and it had not been until the great blizzard of
the early 1880s that the wild game of this country had
been decimated. There would have been wolves to play
havoc with the sheep, for in those days, everyone kept
sheep. There would have been guinea fowl whistling in
the hedgerows, for, in those days, as well, everyone kept
guineas. And the chances were that there would have
been peacocks, geese, ducks, chickens, wandering the
yards. Good horses in the stable, for everyone in those
days placed great emphasis on good horses. And, above
all, the great pride in one's own acreage, in the well-kept
barns, the herds of cattle, the wheat, the corn, the newly
planted orchard. And the old man, himself, he wondered
– what kind of man was old Ned Parker, walking the
path from the house up to the windmill. A stout and
stocky man, perhaps, for the Parkers ran to stocky. An
erect old man, for he'd been four years a soldier in the
Union Army. Walking, perhaps, with his hands clasped
behind his back, and head thrown back to stare up at the
windmill, his present pride and glory.

Grandfather, Thomas asked himself, what happened?
What is this all about? Did you feel belonging as I feel
belonging? Did you feel the openness of this high ridge,
the windswept sense of intimacy, the personality of the
land as I feel it now? Was it here then, as well as now?
And if that should have been the case, as it certainly
must have been, why did you leave?

There was no answer, of course. He knew there would
not be. There was no one now to answer. But even as he
asked the question, he knew that this was a land loaded
with information, with answers if one could only dig
them out. There is something worth knowing here, he

told himself, if one could only find it. The land was ancient. It had stood and watched and waited as ages swept over it, like cloud shadows passing across the land. Since time immemorial, it had stood sentinel above the river and had noted all that had come to pass.

There had been amphibians floundering and bellowing in the river swamps, there had been herds of dinosaurs and those lonely ones that had preyed upon the herds, there had been rampaging titanotheres and the lordly mammoth and the mastodon. There had been much to see and note.

The old black man had said look back, look back beyond the time of man, to the forgotten primal days. To the day, Thomas wondered, when each worshipping dinosaur had swallowed one stone encised with a magic line of cryptic symbols as an earnest that it held faith in a primal god?

Thomas shook himself. You're mad, he told himself. Dinosaurs had no gods. Only men had the intelligence that enabled them to create their gods.

He left the iris patch and paced slowly up the hill, heading for the windmill, following the now nonexistent path that old Ned Parker must have followed more than a hundred years before.

He tilted back his head to look up at the spinning wheel, moving slowly in the gentle morning breeze. So high against the sky, he thought, so high above the world.

The platform of the well was built of hewn oak timbers, weathered by the years, but still as sound as the day they had been laid. The outer edge of them was powdery and crumbling, but the powdering and the crumbling did not go deep. Thomas stopped and flicked at the wood with a fingernail and a small fragment of the oak came free, but beneath it the wood was solid. The timbers would last, he knew, for another hundred years, perhaps several hundred years.

As he stood beside the platform, he became aware of the sound that came from the well. Nothing like a whistle, but a slight moaning, as if an animal somewhere near its bottom were moaning in its sleep. Something alive, he told himself, something moaning gently far beneath the surface, a great heart and a great brain beating somewhere far below in the solid rock.

The brains and hearts of olden dinosaurs, he thought, or the gods of dinosaurs. And brought himself up short. You're at it again, he told himself, unable to shake this nightmare fantasy of the dinosaur. The finding of the heap of gizzard stones must have left a greater mark upon him that he had thought at first.

It was ridiculous on the face of it. The dinosaurs had had dim intellects that had done no more than drive them to the preservation of their own lives and the pro-creation of their kind. But logic did not help; illogic surged within him. No brain capacity, of course, but some other organ – perhaps supplementary to the brain – that was concerned with faith?

He grew rigid with anger at himself, with disgust at such flabby thinking, at a thought that could be little better than the thinking of the rankest cult enthusiast, laced with juvenility.

He left the well and walked up to the track he had followed coming in. He walked along it rapidly, bemused at the paths his mind had taken. The place, he thought, for all its openness, all its reaching toward the sky, all its geographic personality, worked a strange effect upon one. As if it were not of a piece with the rest of the earth, as if it stood apart, wondering, as he thought this, if that could have been the reason all the families left.

He spent the day upon the ridge, covering the miles of it, poking in its corners, forgetting the bemusement and the anger, forgetting even the very strangeness of it, glorying, rather, in the strangeness and that fascinating sense of freedom and of oneness with the sky. The rising wind from the west tugged and pulled at him. The land was clean, not with a washed cleanness but with the clean of a thing that had never been dirty, that had stayed fresh and bright from the day of its creation, untouched by the greasy fingers of the world.

He found the gaping cellar-holes of other farmhouses and squatted near them almost worshipfully, seeking out the lilac clumps, the crumbling remains of vanished fences, the still remaining stretches of earlier paths, now not going anywhere, the flat limestone slabs that had formed doorsteps or patios. And, from these, he formed within his mind the profiles of the families that had lived here for a time, perhaps attracted to it even as he found himself attracted to it, and who, in the end, had fled. He tested the wind and the highness, the antiseptic ancientness and tried to find within them the element of horror that might have brought about their fleeing. But he found no horror; all he found was a rough sort of serenity.

He thought again of the old lady in the rocking chair that day he had sat with her at tea in an old New England house, eating thin-sliced bread and butter. She was touched, of course. She had to be. There was no earthly reason she should want to know so desperately the details of the family house.

He had told her nothing of his investigations. He had reported every now and then by very formal letters to let her know he was still working on the project. But she would not know the story of the Parkers until he had put the manuscript into her clawlike hands. She would find some surprises, he was sure. No horse thieves, no gallows birds, but there had been others she could not have guessed and in whom she could take no pride. If it was pride that she was seeking. He was not sure it was. There had been the medicine-show Parker of the early nineteenth century who had been run out of many towns because of his arrogance and the inferiority of his product. There had been a renegade slave trader in the middle of the century, the barber in an Ohio town who had run off with the wife of the Baptist minister, the desperado who had died in a hail of withering gunfire in a western cattle town. Perhaps, he thought, Aunt Elsie might like the desperado. A strange tribe, this branch of the Parkers, ending with the man who had drilled a well that could have loosed upon the countryside the spawn of ancient evil. And stopped himself at that. You do not know it for a fact, he sternly told himself. You don't even have the smallest ground for slightest speculation. You're letting this place get to you.

The sun was setting when he came back down the track, turning off to go down to the camper parked beside the spring. He had spent the day upon the ridge and he would not spend another. Tomorrow he would leave. There was no reason for staying longer. There might be something here that needed finding, but nothing he could find.

He was hungry, for he had not eaten since breakfast. The fire was dead and he rekindled it, cooked a meal and ate it as the early-autumn dusk crept in. Tired from his day of tramping, he still felt no need of sleep. He sat in the camp chair and listened to the night close down. The eastern sky flushed with the rising moon and down in the hills that rose above the river valley a couple of owls chortled back and forth.

Finally, he rose from the chair and went into the camper to get the bottle. There was some whiskey left and he might as well finish it off. Tomorrow, if he wished, he could buy another. In the camper, he lit the lantern and placed it on the desk. In the light of the lantern, he saw the gizzard stone, where he had left it on the desk top the night before. He picked it up and turned it until he could see the faint insciption on it. He bent forward to try to study the faint line, wondering if he might have mistaken some small imperfection in the stone as writing, feeling a nagging doubt as to the validity of his examination of it the night before. But the cryptic symbols still were there. They were not the sort of tracery that could occur naturally. Was there anyone on earth, he wondered, who could decipher the message on the stone? And even asking it, he doubted it. Whatever the characters might be, they had been graven millions of years before the first thing even faintly resembling man had walked upon the earth. He dropped the stone in his jacket pocket, found the bottle, and went out to the fire.

There was an uneasiness in him, an uneasiness that seemed to hang in the very air. Which was strange, because he had not noted the uneasiness when he had left the fire to go into the camper. It was something that had come in that small space of time he'd spent inside the camper. He studied the darkening terrain carefully, and there was movement out beyond the campfire circle, but it was, he decided, only the movement of trees shaken by the wind. For in the short time since early evening, the wind had shifted to the north and was blowing up a gale. The leaves of the huge cottonwood under which the camper sat were singing, that eerie kind of song that leaves sing in a heavy wind. From the ridge above came the banging clatter of the windmill – and something else as well. A whistle. The well was whistling. He heard the whistle only at intervals, but as he listened more attentively to catch the sound of it, it became louder and consistent, a high, unbroken whistling that had no break or rhythm, going on and on.

Now there was movement, he was certain, beyond the campfire light that could not be accounted for by the thrashing of the trees. There were heavy thumpings and bumpings, as if great ungainly bodies were moving in the dark. He leaped from the chair and stood rigid in the flickering firelight. The bottle slipped from his fingers and he did not stoop to pick it up. He felt the panic rising in him and even as he tried to brush it off, his nerves and muscles tightened involuntarily in an atavistic fear – fear of the unknown, of the bumping in the dark, of the uncanny whistling of the well. He yelled, not at what might be out beyond the campfire, but at himself, what remained of logic, what remained of mind raging at the terrible fear that had gripped his body. Then the logic and the mind succumbed to the fear and, in blind panic, he ran for the camper.

He leaped into the cab, slammed himself into the seat, reached out for the starting key. At the first turn of the key, the motor exploded into life. When he turned on the headlights, he seemed to see the bumping, humping shapes, although even in the light he could not be sure. They were, if they were there at all, no more than heavier shadows among all the other shadows.

Sobbing in haste, he put the engine into gear, backed the camper up the slope and in a semicircle. Then, with it headed up the slope, he pushed the gear to forward. The four-wheel drive responded and, slowly gathering speed, the camper went charging up the hill toward the track down which he had come, past the thumping windmill, only hours before.

The spidery structure of the windmill stood stark against the moon-washed sky. The blades of the rotating wheel were splashes of light, catching and shattering the feeble light of the newly risen moon. Over it all rose the shrieking whistle of the well. The farmer, Thomas remembered, had said that the well whistled only when the wind blew from the north.

The camper reached the track, barely visible in the flare of headlights and Thomas jerked the wheel to follow it. The windmill now was a quarter of a mile away, perhaps less than a quarter mile. In less than a minute, he would be past it, running down the ridge, heading for the safety of another world. For this ridge, he told himself, was not of this world. It was a place set apart, a small wedge of geography that did not quite belong. Perhaps, he thought, that had been a part of its special charm, then when one entered here, he shed the sorrows and the worries of the real world. But, to counter-balance that, he also found something more frightening than the real world would conjure up.

Peering through the windshield, it seemed to Thomas that the windmill had somehow altered, had lost some of its starkness, that it had blurred and changed – that, in fact, it had come alive and was engaging in a clumsy sort of dance, although there was a certain flowing smoothness to the clumsiness.

He had lost some of his fear, was marginally less paralysed with fear than he had been before. For now he was in control, to a certain extent at least, and not hemmed in by horrors from which he could not escape. In a few more seconds, he would be past the windmill, fleeing downwind from the whistle, putting the nightmare all behind him. Putting, more than likely, his imagination all behind him, for the windmill could not be alive, there were no humping shapes . . .

Then he realised that he was wrong. It was not imagination. The windmill was alive. He could see its aliveness more clearly than imagination could have shown it. The structure was festooned and enwrapped by wriggling, climbing shapes, none of which he could see in their entirety, for they were so entangled in their climbing that no one of them could be seen in their entirety. There was about them a drippiness, a loathesomeness, a scaliness that left him gulping in abject terror. And there were, as well, he saw, others of them on the ground surrounding the well, great dark, humped figures that lurched along until they crossed the track.

Instinctively, without any thought at all, he pushed the accelerator to the floorboards and the camper leaped beneath him, heading for the massed bodies. He would crash into them, he thought, and it had been a silly thing to do. He should have tried to go around them. But now it was too late; panic had taken over and there was nothing he could do.

The engine spit and coughed, then slobbered to a halt. The camper rolled forward, came to a staggering stop. Thomas twisted the starter key. The motor turned and coughed. But it would not start. All the dark humps bumped themselves around to look at him. He could see no eyes, but he could feel them looking. Frantically, he cranked the engine. Now it didn't even cough. The damn thing's flooded, said one corner of his mind, the one corner of his mind not flooded by his fear.

He took his hand off the key and sat back. A terrible coldness came upon him – a coldness and a hardness. The fear was gone, the panic gone; all that remained was the coldness and the hardness. He unlatched the door and pushed it open. Deliberately, he stepped down to the ground and moved away from the camper. The windmill, freighted with its monsters, loomed directly overhead. The massed humped shapes blocked the track. Heads, if they were heads, moved back and forth. There was the sense of twitching tails, although he could see no tails. The whistling filled the universe, shrill, insistent, unending. The windmill blades, unhampered by the climbing shapes, clattered in the wind.

Thomas moved forward. 'I'm coming through,' he said, aloud. 'Make way for me. I am coming through.' and it seemed to him that as he walked slowly forward, he was walking to a certain beat, to a drum that only he could hear. Startled, he realised that the beat he was walking to was the creaking of that rocking chair in the old New England house.

Illogic said to him, *It's all that you can do. It's the only thing to do. You cannot run, to be pulled down squealing. It's the one thing a man can do.*

He walked slowly, but deliberately, marching to the slow, deliberate creaking of the rocking chair. 'Make way,' he said. 'I am the thing that came after you.'

And they seemed to say to him, through the shrill whistling of the well, the clatter of the windmill blades, the creaking of the chair, *Pass, strange one. For you carry with you the talisman we gave our people. You have with you the token of your faith.*

Not my faith, he thought. Not my talisman. That's not the reason you do not dare to touch me. I swallowed no gizzard stone.

But you are brother, they told him, *to the one who did.*

They parted, pulled aside to clear the track for him, to make way for him. He glanced to neither left nor right, pretending they were not there at all, although he knew they were. He could smell the rancid, swamp-smell of them. He could feel the presence of them. He could feel the reaching out, as if they meant to stroke him, to pet him as one might a dog or cat, but staying the touch before it came upon him.

He walked the track and left them behind, grouped in their humpiness all about the well. He left them deep in time. He left them in another world and headed for his own, striding, still slowly, slow enough so they would not think that he was running from them, but a bit faster than he had before, down the track that bisected Parker's Ridge.

He put his hand into the pocket of the jacket, his fingers gripping the greasy smoothness of the gizzard stone. The creaking of the chair still was in his mind and he still marched to it, although it was growing fainter now.

Brother, he thought, they said brother to me. And indeed I am. All life on earth is brother and sister and each of us can carry, if we wish the token of our faith.

He said aloud, to that ancient dinosaur that had died so long ago among the tumbled boulders, 'Brother, I am glad to know you. I am glad I found you. Glad to carry the token of your faith.'

The Marathon Photograph

There is no point in putting this account on paper. For
me, a stolid professor of geology, it is an exercise in
futility, eating up time that would be better spent in
working on my long-projected, oft-delayed text on the
Precambrian, for the purpose of which I still am on a
two-quarter leave of absence, which my bank account
can ill afford. If I were a writer of fiction I could make a
story out of it, representing it as no more than a tale of
the imagination, but at least with some chance of placing
it before the public. If I were anything other than a dry-
as-dust college professor, I could write it as a factual
account (which, of course, it would be) and submit it to
one of the so-called fact magazines that deal in raw
sensationalism, with content on such things as treasure
hunts, flying saucers, and the underground – and again
with the good chance that it might see the light of print,
with at least some of the more moronic readers according
it some credence. But a college professor is not supposed
to write for such media and most assuredly would feel the
full weight of academic censure should he do so. There
always is, of course, the subterfuge of writing under an
assumed name and changing the names of those who
appear in the text, but even should I not shrink from this
(which I do) it would offer only poor protection, since at
least part of the story is known to many others and,
accordingly, I could be identified quite easily.

Yet, in spite of all these arguments, I find that I must

write down what happened. White paper covered with
the squiggles of my penmanship may, after a fashion,
serve the function of the confessional, lifting from my
soul and mind the burden of a lonely knowledge. Or it
may be that subconsciously I hope, by putting it down in
a somewhat orderly fashion, to uncover some new understanding or some justification for my action which had
escaped me heretofore. Anyone reading this – although I
am rather certain no one ever will – must at once
perceive that I have little understanding of those psycho-
logical factors that drive me to what must seem a rather
silly task. Yet, if the book on the Precambrian is ever to
be finished, it seems, this account must be finished first.
The ghost of the future must be laid to rest before I
venture into the past.

I find some trouble in determining where to start. My
writing for academic journals, I realise, cannot serve as a
model for this effort. But it does seem to me that the
approach in any writing chore must be logical to some
degree at least, and that the content must be organised in
some orderly fashion. So it appears that a good place to
start might be with the bears.

It had been a bad summer for the bears. The berry
crop had failed and the acorns would not ripen until fall.
The bears dug for roots, ripped open rotten logs to get at
grubs and ants and other insects that might he hidden
there, labored long and furiously to dig out mice and
gophers, or tried, with minimal success, to scoop trout
from the steams. Some of them, driven by their hunger,
drifted out of the hills to nearby tiny towns or lurked in
the vicinity of resorts, coming out at night from their
hiding places to carry out raids upon garbage cans.
These activities created a great furor, with the nightly
locking and barring of doors and windows and an in-
dustrious oiling of guns. There was some shooting, with
one scrawny bruin, a wandering dog, and a cow falling

victims to the hunters. The Division of Wildlife of the State Conservation Department issued the kind of weighty, rather pompous warning that is characteristic of entrenched bureaucracy, recommending that bears be left alone; they were a hungry tribe, consequently out of temper, and could be dangerous.

The accuracy of the warning was borne out in a day or two by the death of Stefan, the caretaker at the Lodge back in the hills, only a half mile or less from the cabin that Neville Piper and I had built a dozen years or more ago, driving up from the university and working on it of weekends. It had taken, for all its modest proportions, a couple of years to build.

I realise that if I were a really skillful writer I'd go on with the story and in the course of telling it weave in all the background information. But I know that if I try it, I will be awkward at it; the writing of geological papers intended for scientific journals is not the kind of thing that trains one for that kind of writing craftmanship. So, rather than attempt it and get all tangled up, it might be a good idea to stop right here and write what I knew at that time about the Lodge.

Actually, I didn't know too much about it, nor did anyone. Dora, who ran the Trading Post, a fanciful name for an old-fashioned general store that stood all by itself where the road into the hills branched off from the valley road, for years had carried deep resentment against the people who occasionally came to the Lodge because she had been able to learn almost nothing of them. About all that she knew was that they came from Chicago, although, when pressed upon the point, she wasn't even sure of that. Dora knew almost all the summer visitors in the hills. I think that over the years she had come to think of them as family. She knew them by their first names and where they lived and how they made a living, plus any other information of interest that might be attached to them. She knew, for example, how for years I had been trying to write my book, and she was quite aware that not only was Neville a famous Greek historian, but that he also was widely known as a photographer of wildlife and nature. She had managed to get hold of three or four of those coffee-table books that had used some of Neville's work and showed them to all comers. She knew all about the honors that had been conferred upon him for his photographic study of asters. She knew about his divorce and his remarriage and how that hadn't worked out, either. And while her accounts of the subject may have been somewhat short of accuracy, they did not lack in detail. She knew I'd never married, and alternately she was enraged at me for my attitude, then sympathetic toward my plight. I never could decide whether it was her rage or her pity that incensed me most. After all, it was none of her damn business, but she made everything her business.

So far as technology is concerned, the hills are a backward place. There is no electricity, no gas, no mail service, no telephones. The Trading Post has a subpostoffice and a telephone, and for this reason, as well as for the groceries and the other items carried on its shelves, it is a sort of central hub for the summer visitors. If you were going to stay for any length of time, you had your mail forwarded, and if you needed a telephone, the Trading Post had the nearest one. It was inconvenient, of course, but few of the visitors minded, for the greater part of them came into the hills to hide away momentarily from the outside world. Most of them came from only a few hundred miles away, but there were some who lived as far away as the East Coast. These visitors flew into Chicago, as a rule, and boarded the Galloping Goose to fly to Pine Bend, about thirty miles from the hills, renting cars to travel the rest of the way. The Galloping Goose was the Northlands Airline, a regional company that served the smaller cities in a four-state area. Despite its ancient equipment, it did a creditable job, usually getting in on time, and with one of the finest safety records of any airline in existence. There was one hazard; if the weather was bad at a certain landing field, the pilot didn't even try to land, but skipped that particular stop. The fields had no lights and there were no towers, and when there was a storm or a field socked in by fog, the pilots took no chances – which may help to explain the excellent safety record. There were many friendly jokes attached to the Galloping Goose, most of them with no basis of truth whatever. For example, it was untrue that at Pine Bend someone had to go out and drive the deer off the runway before a plane could land. Personally, over the years, I developed a very friendly, almost possessive feeling towards the Galloping Goose – not because I used it, for I never did, but because its planes flew on their regular schedules over our cabin. Out fishing, I'd hear one of them approaching and I would stand and watch it pass over, and after a time I found myself sort of anticipating a flight – the way one would watch a clock.

I see that I am wandering. I really started out to tell about the Lodge.

The Lodge was called the Lodge because of all the summer places in the hills it was the largest and the only one that was pretentious in the least. Also, as it turned out, it had been the first. Humphrey Highmore, not Dora, had been the one who told me the most about the Lodge. Humphrey was a ponderous old man who prided himself on being the unofficial historian of Woodman County. He scrabbled out a living of sorts by painting and hanging wallpaper, but he was first and foremost a historian. He pestered Neville every chance he got and was considerably put out because Neville never was able to generate much interest in purely local history.

The Lodge had been built, Humphrey told me, somewhat more than forty years before, long before anyone else had evinced an interest in the hills as a vacation area. All the old-time residents, at the time, thought that whoever was building it was out of his right mind. There was nothing back in those hills but a few trout streams and, in good years, some grouse shooting, although there were years when there weren't many grouse. It was a long way from any proper place, and the land, of course, was worthless. It was too rough to farm, and the timber was so heavy it was no good for pasture, and the land was too rough to harvest timber. Most of it was tax-forfeited land.

And here came this madman, whoever he might be, and spent a lot of money not only to erect the Lodge, but to build five miles of road through the nightmare hills to reach it. Humphrey, who had told me the story on several occasions, always indicated at this point a further source of irritation that perhaps would have been felt most keenly by a devoted historian – no one had ever really learned who this madman was. So far as anyone knew, he had never appeared upon the scene during the time the Lodge and road were being built. All the work had been done by contractors, with the contracts let by letter through a legal firm. Humphrey thought the firm was based in Chicago, but he wasn't sure. Whether the builder ever actually visited the Lodge after it was built was not know, either. People did come to stay in it occasionally, but no one ever saw them come or leave. They never came down to the Trading Post to make any purchases or to pick up mail or make a phone call. The buying that was done or other chores that needed to be performed were done by Stefan, who seemed to be the caretaker, although not even that was certain. Stefan, no last name. Stefan, period. 'Like he was trying to hide something,' Humphrey told me. 'He never talked, and if you asked him anything, he managed not to answer. You'd think a man would tell you his last name if you should ask him. But not Stefan.' On his infrequent trips out from the Lodge, Stefan always drove a Cadillac. Most men usually are willing to talk about their cars, said Humphrey, and a Cadillac was seen seldom enough in these parts that there were a lot of people who would have liked to talk about it, to ask questions about it. But Stefan wouldn't talk about the Cadillac. To Dora and Humphrey he was an irritating man.

It had taken several months, Humphrey said, to get the road into the Lodge built. He explained that at the time he had been off in another part of the county and had not paid much attention to the Lodge, but in later years he had talked with the son of the man who had the contract to build the road. The road as it first was built was good enough for trucks to haul in the material to build the Lodge, but once it had been built the track was fairly well torn up by truck traffic, so there had been a second contract let to bring the road back to first-class condition. 'I suppose a good road was needed for the Cadillac,' Humphrey said. 'Even from the first it was a Cadillac. Not the same Cadillac, of course, although I'm not sure how many.'

Humphrey always had plenty of stories to tell; he bubbled with them. He had a pathological need to communicate, and he was not bothered too much by repetition. He had two favorite topics. One, of course, was the mystery of the Lodge – if it really was a mystery. Humphrey thought it was. His other favourite was the lost mine. If there was a lost mine, it would have had to have been a lead mine. There were lead deposits all through the area. Humphrey never admitted it was a lead mine; he made it sound as if it might be gold.

As I gathered it, the lost-mine story had been floating around for a long time before Humphrey fastened hold of

it. That there was such a story was no great surprise –
there are few areas that do not possess at least one
legendary lost mine or buried treasure. Such stories are
harmless local myths and at times even pleasant ones,
but at least subconsciously they are recognised for what
they are, and it is seldom that anyone pays much
attention to them. Humphrey did, however, pay
attention to the story; he ran it down relentlessly, chasing
after clues, reporting breathlessly to anyone who would
listen to him his latest scrap of information or imagined
information.

On that July morning when it all began I drove down
to the Trading Post to buy some bacon and pick up our
mail. Neville had planned to make the trip so that I
could get started on the textbook project, but after
several rainy days the sun had come out and during all
the rainy spell he'd been praying for a few hours of
sunlight to photograph a stand of pink lady's slippers
that were in bloom a short distance below the bridge just
beyond the Lodge. He had been down there for several
days in the rain, floundering around, getting soaked to
the skin and taking pictures. The pictures had been fine,
as his pictures always are. Still, he needed sunlight for
the best result.

When I left, he'd had all his equipment spread out on
the kitchen table, selecting what he'd need to take along.
Neville is a fussy photographer – I guess most photographers are, the ones who are interested in their work.
He had more gadgets than you can imagine, and each of
those gadgets, as I understand it, is built for a specific
task. It's his fussiness, I suppose, and all those gadgets
he has collected, that make him the outstanding photographer he is.

When I arrived at the Trading Post, Humphrey was
there, sitting all by himself in one of the several chairs
pulled up around the cold heating stove that stood in the

center of the store. He had the look of someone who was waiting for a victim, and I didn't have it in my heart to disappoint him. So after buying the bacon and picking up the mail, I went back to the stove and sat down in the chair next to him.

He didn't waste any time in idle chatter; he got right down to business.

'I've told you, I think,' he said, 'about the lost mine.'

'Yes,' I said. 'We have discussed it several times.'

'You recall the main thrust of the story,' he said. 'How it was supposed to have been discovered by two deserters from Fort Crawford who were hiding in the hills. That would have been back in the 1830s or so. As the story went, the mine was discovered in a cave – that is, there was a cave, and cropping out in the cave was a drift of mineral, very rich, I understand.'

'What I've never been able to figure out about it,' I said, 'is even if they found the mine, why they should have bothered to try to work it. It would have been lead, wouldn't it?'

'Yes,' said Humphrey, somewhat reluctantly, 'I suppose it would have been.'

'Think of the problem of getting it out,' I said. 'I suppose they would have had to smelt the ore and cast it into pigs and then bring in pack animals to get out the pigs. And all the time with the Army with an eye out for them.'

'I suppose you're right,' said Humphrey, 'but there's magic in a mine. The very idea of finding riches in the earth is somehow exciting. Even if there's no way to work it . . .'

'You've made your point,' I said. 'I think I understand.'

'Well, in any case,' said Humphrey, 'they never really worked it. They started to, but something happened and they pulled out. Left the country and were never seen again. They are supposed to have told someone that they cut logs to conceal the cave mouth and shoveled dirt over the logs. To hide the mine from anyone else, you understand. Figuring maybe some day they'd come back and work it. I've often wondered, if all this is true, why they never did come back. You know, Andrew, I think that now I have the answer. Not only the answer, but the first really solid evidence that the old story is not a myth. I think as well that I may be able to identify that hitherto unknown person who got the story started.'

'Some new evidence?' I asked.

'Yes, quite by chance,' he said. 'Knowing I am interested in the history of this area, people often bring me things they find – old things, like letters or clippings from old newspapers. You know the kind of stuff.'

I said, indeed, I did. He had me interested, but even if I hadn't been I'd let him get started on it and I had to hear him out.

'The other day,' he said, 'a man from the eastern part of the county brought me a journal he'd found in an old box in the attic. The farmhouse had been built by his grandfather, say a hundred years or more ago, and the farm had stayed in the family ever since. The man who brought me the journal is the present owner of it. The journal apparently had been written by his great-grandfather, the father of the man who originally settled on the farm. This great-grandfather, for several years when he was a young man, had run a trading post up on the Kickapoo, trading with the Sauks and Foxes who still were in the area. Not much of a business, apparently, but he made a living out of it. Did some trapping on his own and that helped. The journal covers a period of about three years, from 1828 well into '31. Entries for almost every day, sometimes only a single sentence, but entries. At other times several pages filled, summarising events of the past few weeks, previously only mentioned sketchily or not at all . . .'

'There was mention of a mine?' I asked, getting a bit impatient. Left to himself, he could have rambled on for hours.

'Towards the end of it,' he said. 'August of '31, I think. I can't recall the date. Two men, who I take to have been the deserters, came to the post late one evening, seeking food and shelter. It had been some time since our journalist had seen another white man, and I would suspect they made a night of it, sitting up and drinking. They would not have told him what they did if they'd not had a few too many. They didn't out and out say they were deserters, but he suspected it. The fort authorities had asked him some time before to be on the lookout for them. But it appears he had been having some trouble with the military and was not about to help the fort. So it would have been safe enough for the two to have told him they were deserters, although apparently they didn't. They told him about the mine, however, and pinpointed it close enough so he could guess that it was somewhere in these hills. They told him the story that has come down to us, little changed. How they cut the logs to cover up the cave mouth before they left.

'But they told him something else that has not come down to us – why they fled the country. Something scared them, something they found in the mine. They didn't know what it was; they never got close enough to it to find out. It ticked at them, they said; it sat there and ticked at them. Not regular, like a clock, but erratically, like it might be trying to talk with them, they said. Warning them, perhaps. Threatening them. When they first encountered it, apparently, they went out into the open, like a shot, scared stiff. It must have been an eerie sort of feeling. Then getting a little over it and feeling sheepish about being scared so easily, they went back into the cave, and as soon as they stepped inside it, the ticking started up again. That did it. You must re-

member that more than a century ago, when all this
happened, men were somewhat more inclined to superstitions than they are now, more easily frightened by
what might appear to be supernatural. I remember a fine
old Irish gentleman who lived on a farm near my father's
farm. When I was a small boy he was well into his
seventies, and I, of course, did not hear his story of the
graveyard ghost. But in later years I did hear my father
tell it many times. It appears that one night, driving
home in a cart that he habitually used in his travels
about the countryside, he saw or thought he saw a white-
sheeted ghost in the graveyard only a few miles from his
home. Ever after that, when he was out at night and
coming home, upon approaching the cemetery he would
whip up his horse and go past the cemetery as fast as
good horseflesh could carry him.'

'It was after the second ticking incident that they left,'
I said.

'Yes, apparently. The journal's not entirely clear. The
keeper of the journal was no great writer, you must
understand. His syntax leaves much to be desired and
his spelling takes a moderate amount of deciphering.
But, yes, it seems they did light out after that second
incident. The wonder is, frightened as they seemed to be,
that they took the time to conceal the cave.'

The screen door banged and I turned around to see
who it was. It was Neville. He stopped just inside the
door and stood there, straight and calm, the way he
always is, but a bit stiffer in his straightness, it seemed to
me, than was usual.

'Dora,' he said to the woman behind the counter, 'I
wonder if you'd phone the sheriff for me.'

I got up from the chair. 'The sheriff?' I asked. 'What
do you want the sheriff for?'

He didn't answer me immediately. He spoke to Dora.
'Tell him that Stefan, up at the Lodge, is dead. Killed by

a bear, it seems. Just below the bridge this side of the Lodge. The one over Killdeer Creek.'

Humphrey was on his feet by this time. 'Are you sure he's dead?' he asked.

'Reasonably certain,' said Neville. 'I didn't touch him, of course. But his throat's ripped out and it would seem his neck is broken. There are bear tracks all about. The slope down to the stream is muddy from the rains and the tracks are clearly seen.'

Dora was on the phone. Neville said to her, 'I'm going back. I don't think he should be left alone.'

'The bear won't come back,' said Humphrey. 'Granted, they are hungry. But if he didn't eat him at the time . . .'.

'Nevertheless,' said Neville, 'I am going back. It's not decent to leave him there any longer than is necessary. Andy, do you want to follow me?'

'Certainly,' I said.

Humphrey dealt himself in. 'I'll wait for the sheriff,' he said. 'When he comes along, I'll flag him down and ride along with him.'

Neville and I got back to the bridge half an hour or so before the sheriff and Humphrey showed up. We parked our cars and walked down below the bridge. And there, only a few yards from the creek, was Stefan.

'We better sit down up here,' said Neville. 'There's nothing we can do but watch. We don't want to go tracking up the place. There's not much doubt what happened, but the sheriff will want the area to be left undisturbed.'

We found adjacent boulders and sat down upon them. Neville glanced at the sky. It was clouding up again. 'There goes my chance for pictures,' he said. 'And those blooms only have another day or two to go. Besides . . .'

He said that 'besides' and then he stopped. As if there were something he had been about to tell me and then decided not to. I didn't question him. Maybe one of the reasons we've been friends so long is that we do not question one another.

'There are some good trout in that pool just below the bridge,' I said. 'One of these days I'm going after them. I picked up some new flies before I drove up. Maybe they'll do the job.'

'I have to go back to the university,' said Neville. 'Tonight, if I can. Tomorrow morning at the latest.'

I was surprised. 'I thought you were staying for another week or two.'

'Something came up,' he said.

We sat and passed away the time with inconsequential talk until the sheriff arrived. As I looked at Stefan sprawled out on the stream bank, it seemed to me that he looked smaller than I remembered him. I found myself wondering if life added an extra dimension to a man. Take life away, would the man grow smaller? He lay with his face up to the sky, and there were flies and other insects crawling on his face. The position of his head concealed his torn-out throat, but there were bright specks of red still on the leaves and forest loam, blood that as yet had not turned to brown. I tried to make out the bear tracks that Neville had mentioned, but I was too distant from the body to make them out.

The sheriff turned out to be a genial man, soft-spoken, unofficious. He was a big man, rather fleshy. He looked like the TV stereotype of a hick-town sheriff, but he didn't talk or act like one. He came clambering down the bank, with Humphrey following. He spoke to Neville, 'You are Mr Piper. I think we met several years ago. And you must be Mr Thornton. I don't think we've ever met. You're a geologist, I understand.'

We shook hands and the sheriff said to Neville, 'You asked Dora to call. She said you were the one who found the body.'

'I was on my way to photograph some flowers,' said Neville. 'He's just the way I found him. I touched nothing. It was apparent he was dead. There were bear tracks.'

'The ambulance will be along any minute now,' the sheriff said. 'Let's have a look.'

We went down and had a look. There was nothing much to see. It was rather horrible, of course, but the body, the man reduced by the absence of life, was so small and insignificant that it had little impact. Balanced against the brawling stream, the sweeping extent of birch and pine, the deep silence of the wilderness, the fact of human death canceled out to very little.

'Well,' the sheriff said, 'I guess I better have a closer look. This is something that I always hate to do, but it goes with the job.'

He bent over the body and began going through the pockets. He looked through the pockets of the jacket and the shirt and had to roll the body a little to explore the back pockets of the trousers. He came up with nothing.

He straightened up and looked at us. 'That's funny,' he said. 'Nothing. Not even a billfold. No papers. He had no pocketknife; most men carry pocketknives. I don't think I've ever run into that before. Even the filthiest old bum, dead in some back alley, always has something on him – an old letter, a photograph, faded and torn, from long ago, a piece of twine, a knife, something. But this one is absolutely clean.'

He stepped away, shaking his head. 'I can't figure it,' he said. 'Stands to reason a man would have something on him.' He looked at Neville. 'You didn't go through his pockets, did you? No, of course you didn't. I don't know why I asked.'

'You're right,' Neville said. 'I didn't.'

We went back to the road. The sheriff played a dirty trick on Humphrey, and perhaps there was justice in that because Humphrey really had no right to be there.

'I think', the sheriff said, 'we'd better go up to the Lodge.'

'I doubt there's anyone around,' I said. 'For the last couple of days I've seen no one there, not even Stefan.'

'I think, anyhow, we should have a look,' the sheriff said. 'Just in case there should be someone. Somebody should be notified. Perhaps Humphrey won't mind staying here to flag down the ambulance.'

Humphrey did mind, naturally, but there was nothing he could do about it. Here was the chance to go up to the Lodge, probably to go inside it, and he was being counted out. But he did what he had to do with fairly good grace and said that he would stay.

Passing by the Lodge, of course, one could see that it was a massive structure, half camouflaged by native trees and planted shrubbery. But it was not until one drove up to it, going up the driveway that led to the detached garage that housed the Cadillac, that an adequate idea could be gained of the size of it. From the driveway it became apparent that its true dimensions, as seen from the road, were masked by the fact that it crouched against the hill that rose back of it. By some strange trick of perspective it seemed from the road to be dwarfed by the hill.

The sheriff got out of his car as we drove our cars back of his and parked. 'Funny,' said the sheriff. 'In all these years I have never been here.'

I was thinking the same thing. On a number of occasions, driving past, I had waved to Stefan, if he happened to be out, but I had never stopped. Sometimes Stefan waved back, most of the time he didn't.

The garage door was open and the Cadillac parked inside. It seemed to me, as I looked at it, that there was a strangeness to the garage. Then, quite suddenly, I realised what the strangeness was. Except for the Cadillac, the garage was empty; it had not been used as a storage catch-all, the fate of most garages.

A flight of flagstone steps ran up from the driveway to a terrace and the narow strip of level ground that lay in front of the house. The lawn was intended to be gay, with garden umbrellas, but the gaiety fell a little short, the canvas torn by the wind and faded by the sun.

No one was about. More than that, the place – the house, the lawn, all of it – had an empty feel to it. It felt like a place that never had been lived in, as if it had been built those forty years ago and then been allowed to stand, to age and weather, with no one ever standing underneath its roof. It was a strange sensation and I wondered what was the matter with me that I should be thinking it. I knew that I was wrong. Stefan had done a lot of living here, and occasionally there had been others.

'Well,' the sheriff said, 'I suppose we should go up and see if anyone is home.' I sensed the sheriff felt uncomfortable. I felt uncomfortable myself, as if, somehow, I were an unwelcome guest, as if I'd come to a party, the kind of party that you simply do not crash, without an invitation. All these years the people of this house (whoever they might be) had made it a point of honor that they wished to be left alone, and here we were, invading their fiercely protected privacy, using a tragedy as a pretext.

The sheriff went heavy-footed up the flagstone stairs, with Neville and me following close behind. We came out on a stone patio that led up to the front door. The sheriff rapped on the door. When there was no answer, he pounded on it. I think that all he was doing was going through the motions; he had sensed as well as I had that there was no one there.

He put his hand on the latch and pressed it with his thumb. The door came open and he stuck his head inside. 'Anyone home?' he asked, and then, scarcely waiting for an answer, went on in.

The door opened on a large room; I suppose you

would call it the living room, although it was larger than any living room I had ever seen. A lounge would have described it better. The windows facing the road were heavily draped and the place was dark. There were chairs scattered all about, and a monstrous stone fireplace was opposite the windows. But I only glimpsed these things, for standing in the middle of the room, in almost the exact center of it, stood an object that caught my gaze and held it.

The sheriff shuffled slowly forward. 'What the hell is that?' he rumbled.

It was some sort of transparent box standing on a platform elevated a foot or so above the floor. A framework of what appeared to be metal held the box in place. Inside the box were unsupported green strips, like the yardage stripes that mark off a football field. But the stripes didn't run the way they would on a football field. They were canted at all angles and were of no uniform length. Some of them were short, others long, some of them had zigzags in them. Scattered amid the markings, with no particular pattern, were a number of glowing red and blue dots.

The sheriff stopped when he got to the box and stood looking down on it. He asked, gently, 'Mr Piper, have you ever seen anything like this?'

'Never,' Neville said.

I squatted down, squinting at the box, looking for any sign of wires on which the colored dots might be strung. There was no sign of wires. I poked a finger at the box and struck something hard. Not glass; I would have known the feel of glass. This was something else. I tried several other places and each time the hardness stopped my probing finger.

'What do you make of it, Mr Thornton?' asked the sheriff.

I made a stupid answer. 'It isn't glass,' I said.

Suddenly one of the blue dots changed position. It didn't move from one position to another; it jumped so fast I couldn't see it move. It was at one place and suddenly it was at another place, some three or four inches from where it had been.

'Hey,' I said, 'the damn thing works!'

'A game of some sort,' the sheriff said, uncertainly.

'I wouldn't know,' said Neville. 'There is no evidence upon which to speculate.'

'I suppose not,' said the sheriff. 'Funny setup, though.'

He moved across the room to the windows, started fumbling at the drapes. 'Got to get some light in here,' he said.

I stayed squatting, watching the box. None of the other dots moved.

'Four feet, I'd say,' said Neville.

'Four feet?'

'The box. Four feet square. A cube. Four feet on each side.'

I agreed with him. 'Close to it,' I said.

The sheriff got the drapes open and daylight poured into the room. I got up from my crouch and looked around. The place had a barren look. There was carpeting on the floor. Chairs. Sofas. End tables. Candelabra with wilted candles in them. The fireplace. But no paintings on the walls. No figurines on the fireplace mantel. No small pieces at all. Just the furniture.

'It looks,' said Neville, 'as if no one ever quite finished moving in.'

'Well,' said the sheriff, 'let's get to work. Let's see if we can find anything that will give us a clue to who should be notified of Stefan's death.'

We went through the place. It didn't take us long. All the other rooms were as barren as the lounge. Necessary furniture. That was all. Not a single scrap of paper. Nothing.

Out on the driveway, the sheriff shrugged in resignation. 'It seems unbelievable,' he said.

'What do you do now?' I asked.

'The county registrar of deeds can tell me who owns
the place.'

It was almost noon by the time Neville and I got back
to the cabin. I started to fry some eggs and bacon. I had
the bacon in the pan when Neville stopped me. 'Don't
bother with it now,' he said. 'We can eat a little later.
There's something I have to show you.'

His voice was more tense that I had ever heard it.

'What's the trouble, Neville?'

'This,' he said. He reached into his jacket pocket, took
something out of it, placed it on the kitchen table. It was
a cube, perhaps four inches to the side. It appeared to be
translucent.

'Take a look at it,' he said. 'Tell me what you make of
it.'

I picked it up. It was heavier than I expected. I
weighed it in my hand, puzzled by it.

'Look at it, he said. 'Look into it. Bring it up close to
your face and look inside it. That's the only way to see it.'

At first I saw nothing. Then I brought it closer to my
eyes and there, captured inside of it, I could see what
appeared to be an ancient battle scene. The figures were
small, but lifelike and in full color. There was artistry in
the cube; whoever had fabricated it had been a master of
his craft.

I saw that not only were there warlike figures, but a
background as well – a level plain, and in the distance a
body of water and off to the right some hills.

'Beautiful,' I said. 'Where did you get it?'

'Beautiful? Is that all you can say?'

'Impressive,' I said, 'if you like that better. But you
didn't answer me. Where did you get it?'

'It was lying beside Stefan's body. He'd been carrying

it in the pocket of his jacket, more than likely. The bear had ripped the pocket.'

I handed the cube back to him. 'Strange thing,' I said, 'for a man to be carrying about.'

'Exactly,' Neville said. 'My thought exactly. It had a strange look to it. Not like plastic, not like glass. You've noticed?'

'Yes,' I said. 'Come to think of it, a strange feel, too. A hardness, but no texture to the hardness. Like that box in the center of the room back at the Lodge.'

'Even facing the fact of death,' said Neville, 'startled by the fact of human death, I still was fascinated by the cube lying there beside the body. It is strange how one reacts to shock. I suppose that often we may fasten our attention on some trivial matter, not entirely disassociated from the shock, but not entirely a part of it, either, in an unconscious effort to lessen the impact that might be too great if allowed to come in all at once. By accepting the shock gradually, it becomes acceptable. I don't know, I'm not enough of a psychologist to know, no psychologist at all, of course. But there was the cube and there was Stefan, and as I looked at the cube it seemed to me, rather illogically, that the cube was more important than Stefan. Which, I suppose, is understandable, for Stefan, all these years, had been an object rather than a person, someone that we waved to as we drove past but almost never spoke to, a man one never really met face to face.

'This may all seem strange to you, Andy, and I am a bit surprised myself, for until this moment I have not really considered how I felt when I found the body, never sorted out my reactions. So, to get on with it, I picked up the cube, which I am aware I should not have done, and holding it in my hand and turning it to try to determine what it was, I saw a glint of color from inside it, so I lifted it closer to look at it and saw what you saw just now. And having seen it, there was no question in my mind at all of dropping it back where I found it. I've never been more shaken in my life. I stood there, with the cold sweat breaking out on me, shaking life a leaf . . .'

'But, Neville, why?' I asked. 'I'll admit it is a clever thing, a beautiful piece of work, but . . .'

'You mean you didn't recognise it?'

'You mean the picture in the cube? Why should I?'

'Because it is a photograph of the Battle of Marathon.'

I gasped. 'A photograph? Marathon! How can you know? You are going dotty, Neville.'

'I know because I know the Plain of Marathon,' he said. 'I spent three weeks there two years ago – remember? Camping on the field. Tramping up and down the battlefield. Trying to get the feel of it. And I did get the feel of it. I walked the line of battle. I traced the Persians' flight. I lived that goddamn battle, Andy. There were times, standing in the silence, I could hear the shouting.'

'But you said a photograph. That thing's not any photograph. There's not a camera made . . .'

'I know, but look at this.' He handed back the cube. 'Have another look,' he said.

I had another look. 'There's something wrong,' I said. 'There isn't any water, and there was before. There was a lake off in the distance.'

'Not a lake,' said Neville. 'The Bay of Marathon. Now you are seeing hills, or perhaps a distant marsh. And there is still a battle.'

'A hill,' I said. 'Not too big a hill. What the hell is going on?'

'Turn it. Look through another face.'

I turned it. 'A marsh this time. Way off. And a sort of swale. A dry creek bed.'

'The Charadra,' said Neville. 'A stream. Really two streams. In September, when the battle was fought, the streams no longer ran. The beds were dry. You're looking along the route the Persians fled. Look to your right. Some pine trees.'

'They look like pines.'

'The Schoenia. Pines growing on a sandy beach between the marsh and the sea. The Persian boats are pulled up on that beach, but you can't see them.'

I put the cube back on the table. 'What kind of gag is this?' I asked, half angrily. 'What are you trying to prove?'

He almost pleaded with me. 'I told you, Andy. I'm not trying to prove anything at all. That cube is a photograph of Marathon, of the battle that was fought almost twenty-five centuries ago. I don't know who photographed it or how it was photographed, but I am certain that is what it is. It's no snap judgement on my part. I know. I have examined it more closely than you have. After you left for the Trading Post I decided that instead of driving my car, I'd walk down to the bridge. It's only half a mile or so. It was a fine morning and I felt like a walk. So when I found Stefan I had to come back here to get the car, and I must confess I did not drive to the Trading Post immediately. I know I should have, but I was so excited about the cube – I was fairly sure what it was, but not absolutely certain, the way I am now – and a half hour one way or the other meant nothing whatsoever to Stefan any more. So I took the time to have a good look at the cube and I used a glass on it. Here,' he said, digging around in his pocket, taking out a reading glass. 'Here, use this. The picture doesn't break up with magnification. Those are no toy figures in there, no fabrications, no clever make-believes. They are flesh-and-blood men. Look at the expressions on their faces. Note that details become clearer.'

He was right. Under the glass, the details were sharper, the faces became more human. The beards were not pasted-on beards, not painted-on beards; they were really beards. One Greek hoplite, his mouth open in a shout, had a missing front tooth, and little beads of blood had oozed out of a minor bruise across one cheek.

'Somewhere,' said Neville, 'there is a projector, or whatever it is called. You drop the cube into it and the scene is reproduced. You are standing in the middle of the battle, in a frozen thousandth-second of the battle. . . '

'But there is no such thing,' I said.

'Neither is there a camera that would take a photograph of this sort. It's not only a three-dimensional photograph but an all-angles photograph. Look through one face of it and you see the bay, look through another and you see the marsh. Rotate it through three hundred and sixty degrees and you see the battle all around you. You see it all as it was happening in that thousandth of a second.'

I put the cube and the reading glass back on the table. 'Now, listen,' I said. 'You say this had fallen out of Stefan's pocket. Tell me this – how did Stefan get it?'

'Andy, I don't know. First we'd have to know who Stefan was. Tell me what you know about Stefan. Tell me what you know about the other people who come to the Lodge.'

'I don't know a thing about Stefan or the others,' I said. 'Nor do you. Nor does anyone else.'

'Remember,' Neville reminded me, 'how when the sheriff looked for identification on Stefan's body, he found nothing. No billfold. No scrap of paper. Nothing. How could a man get by without a social security card? Even if he had no other identification . . .'

'He might not have wanted to be identified,' I said. 'He carried nothing so that if something happened to him, there'd be no way for anyone to know who he was.'

'The same thought crossed my mind,' said Neville.

'And the Lodge. It was as clean of paper as Stefan's body.'

I had been standing all this time, but now I sat down at the table. 'Maybe it's time,' I said, 'that we start saying out loud some of the things we have been thinking. If that cube is what you say it is, it means that someone with greater technical skills than we have has traveled in time to take the photograph. It couldn't be an artifact. Back when Marathon was fought no one had ever dreamed of the possibility of even a simple photograph. No one from the present time could take the kind of photograph there is in the cube. So we've got two factors – time travel and time travel done by someone from the future, where an advanced technology might make that photograph possible.'

Neville nodded. 'That has to be the answer, Andy. But you'll not find a responsible physicist who'll concede even the faintest hope that time travel is possible. And if it should be, some time in the future, why should the travelers be here? There's nothing here that could possibly attract them.'

'A hideout,' I said. 'When the Lodge was built, forty years ago, these hills were a good hideout.'

'One thing puzzles me,' said Neville. 'The emptiness of the Lodge. If you were traveling in time, wouldn't you bring back some artifacts? Wouldn't you want something to put up on the mantel?'

'It might be only a stopping place. A place to spend the night every now and then.'

He reached out and took the cube and glass. 'One thing bothers me, he said. 'I should have turned this over to the sheriff.'

'What the world for?' I asked. 'It would only confuse him more, and he's confused enough already.'

'But it's evidence.'

'Evidence, hell,' I said. 'This is no murder. There's no

question what did Stefan in. There's no mystery to it; there's nothing to be solved.'

'You don't blame me, Andy, for wanting to keep it? It's not mine, I know. I have no right to it.'

'If it's what you think it is,' I said, 'you have more right to it than anyone I know. Four studies in the *Journal of Hellenic Studies*, all on Marathon . . .'

'Only three on Marathon, he said. 'One of them concerned the pre-historic Danube Thoroughfare. Some of the bronzes found there seemed to have some connection with Troy. There have been times when I have had some regrets about that paper. Since then I've told myself I wandered somewhat far afield.'

He dropped the cube back into his pocket. 'I might as well get started,' he said. 'I want to reach the university before nightfall. There are hundreds of color slides in my files, taken on the plain of Marathon, and I want to make some comparison checks. Also I want to get some greater magnification than this reading glass affords.'

He stood up, hesitating for a moment. 'You want to come with me, Andy? We could be back in a few days.'

I shook my head. 'I have to get down to work,' I said. 'If I don't get that damn book written this time around, I'll never write it.'

He went into his bedroom and came out with his briefcase.

I stood in the cabin door and watched him drive off. He'd get no sleep this night, I knew. Once back in his office, he'd spend the night working with the photograph of Marathon. I was surprised to find how easy it had become to think of it as a photograph of Marathon. I had come to accept, I realised, what Neville said about it. If there was anyone who would know, I told myself, he would be the one. Neville Piper was among the half dozen men in the world who could be regarded as experts on the Persian campaign of 490 BC. If he said it was Marathon, I stood ready to believe him.

I went out on the porch and sat down in a chair, looking out over the tangled wilderness of the hills. I knew I shouldn't be sitting there. I had an attaché case and a whiskey carton, both filled with notes and half-written chapters, some of them only roughed out and others only needing polishing and checking. I had a brand-new ream of paper and I'd had the typewriter cleaned and oiled – and here I sat out on the porch, staring off into nothing.

But somehow I couldn't make myself get up and go in to work. I couldn't get Stefan or any of the rest of it out of my mind – Stefan, the cube, Stefan's empty pockets, and the empty Lodge, empty of everything except that incredible contraption that the sheriff had thought might be some sort of game. Thinking about it, I was fairly certain it wasn't any game, although, for the life of me, I couldn't imagine what it was.

I sat there stupid, not moving, not wanting to move, sitting there trying to absorb and put together all the strange happenings, listening with half an ear to the sound of wind in the pines that grew just down the hill, the shrill chirring of a startled chipmunk, the squalling of a jay.

Then I became aware of another sound, a distant sound, a droning that steadily grew louder, and I knew it was the noon flight of the Galloping Goose, heading north after stopping at Pine Bend. I got out of my chair and went into the yard, waiting for the plane to come over the treetops. When it showed up it seemed to be flying lower than it usually did, and I wondered if there might be something wrong, although, except for the lower-than-usual altitude, it seemed to be all right. Then, when it was almost directly above me, something apparently did happen. Suddenly the plane, which had been flying level, perhaps actually climbing, although from the ground that would not have been immediately apparent – suddenly the plane went into a bank, dipping one wing and raising the other, and watching it, I had for an instant the distinct impression that it had shuddered. It banked and seemed to wobble, as if it might be staggering. Then, just as it disappeared above the tree-tops, it seemed to right itself and go on as before.

It all had happened so swiftly that I really had seen nothing that I could pin down. Somehow, however, I had the impression that the plane had hit something, although what might be up there to hit I could not imagine. It seemed to me I had read somewhere about planes coming to grief by running into flocks of birds. But that, I remembered, almost always happened on approach or takeoff. Despite the fact that the Galloping Goose had appeared to be flying lower than usual, I realised it probably had been flying too high for birds to be a hazard.

I had glanced down and now, for some reason I don't remember, perhaps for no reason at all, I glanced up at the sky and saw a dark dot hanging almost directly over me. As I watched it got larger, and I could see that it was something falling. It was wobbling about as if it might be tumbling in its fall. From the distance that I viewed it, it looked remarkably like a suitcase, and the thought occurred to me that a piece of luggage may have fallen or been thrown from the plane. Then I realised the improbability of throwing anything from a plane in flight, and realised, as well, that if a cargo hatch had popped open, there'd be more than one piece of luggage falling to the ground.

The whole thing was ridiculous, of course, but it didn't seem ridiculous while I stood there watching the flapping, tumbling whatever-it-was falling toward the ground. Afterward it did seem ridiculous, but not at that time.

For a moment it seemed to be rushing straight down

upon me. I even took a couple of steps to one side so it wouldn't hit me, before I saw that it would come to earth a short distance down the slope below the cabin.

It came crashing down, brushing through the branches of a maple tree, and when it hit the ground it made a soggy thud. In the last few seconds before it hit the tree I could see it was not a piece of luggage. It was hard to make out what it was, but it did look something like a saddle, and of all the things a man would expect to come falling from the sky a saddle would have been the last upon the list.

When I heard it hit, I went running down the slope and there, in a dry ravine below the road, I found it — and it was a saddle, although no kind of saddle I had ever seen before. But it did have stirrups and a seat and what I took to be an adaptation of a saddle horn. It was scratched up a bit, but it really wasn't damaged much. It had fallen in a deep drift of leaves, and the leaves had cushioned its fall. There was, I saw, a rather deep dent in the saddle horn, if that was what it was.

It was heavy, but I managed to hoist it on one shoulder and went puffing and panting up the slope. Back at the cabin I dumped it on the porch floor and it lay all humped up, but when I straightened it out there was no doubt that it was a saddle. The seat was wide and ample and the stirrups were cinched up to the right length for an ordinary man. The horn rose somewhat higher than one would find in an ordinary saddle and was considerably larger and flattened on the top, with what seemed to be control buttons set into its face. The entire structure of the horn was shaped like an elongated box. The saddle was constructed of a good grade of heavy leather, and from the feel of it the frame was made of metal. But leather covered all of it and no metal could be seen. Attached to the forward saddle skirts were two closed saddlebags.

I squatted on the floor beside the saddle and my fingers itched to open up the bags, but I didn't do it for a time. I squatted there and tried to fight down the thought that had popped into my head – not that I wanted to do away with it, to banish it, but rather to bring it down to proper perspective, carve it down in size a bit.

Now let's be logical, I told myself. Let's put down the facts we have. First there is a saddle and the saddle is a fact. It is something one can see and touch. It fell out of the sky and that is another fact – for I had seen it fall. It had fallen after the Galloping Goose had gone through a rather strange maneuver – and that probably could be better listed as an observation rather than a fact.

It all seemed clear to me. The saddle had been up there in the sky and the Galloping Goose had come along and collided with it. After the collision the saddle had fallen from the sky. But, I cautioned myself, I could not be sure of that. I could be sure the saddle had fallen from the sky, but I couldn't be positively sure the plane had caused the fall. Fairly sure, of course, but not entirely so.

Questions rattled in my mind, and on the heel of questions, answers. I pushed both the questions and the answers back and stayed looking at the saddlebags. They lay quite flat, and there was no bulge to them. Although, I told myself, there might be something in them. It wouldn't need to be too much. A clue was all I needed. A clue that would give some support to that one big answer roaring in my brain.

I hunkered down and opened up the first bag. There was nothing in it. I opened the second bag and there was nothing in it, either. Empty – as empty as Stefan's pockets, as empty as the Lodge.

I got up and staggered to the chair and sat weakly in it. The saddle sprawled upon the porch floor and I tried not to look at it.

A time machine, I asked myself – a traveling time machine? You got into the saddle and rose up in the air, then you turned it on and went where you wished in time. But, hell, I told myself, it wouldn't work. Even if you could blind yourself to the impossibility of time travel, there still were a dozen easy reasons why it wouldn't work. I must be insane, I told myself, to even think about it. But tell me, said that mocking, illogical portion of my mind that I didn't even know I had – tell me this, what would a saddle be doing up there in the sky?

I got down on the porch floor on all fours and looked the saddle over. I examined it inch by inch. Hoping, I suppose, for an impression somewhere in the leather which would read: TEXAS SADDLE AND LEATHER CORP, HOUSTON, or something of the sort, anything at all to take my imagination off the hook. I found nothing. There was no imprint or tag to tell the saddle's origin. I felt cold feet walking on my spine. I picked up the saddle and took it in the cabin, tossed it on the floor of the closet off my bedroom and shut the door. Then, halfway back to the porch, I turned around and went back again and threw a pair of trousers and an old sweatshirt over the saddle so it would be hidden. I went back to the porch and sat there, thinking I should get at the book but knowing I'd have to wait for a while before I would get to it. I tried to watch the birds and chipmunks and the other creatures that skittered about the woods, but couldn't seem to work up too much interest in them. I thought about going fishing but decided not to. After a while I cooked some eggs and bacon and, after eating, went out on the porch again.

About three o'clock the sheriff drove up, parked his car and came up on the porch to sit with me.

'I'm not getting anywhere,' he said. 'I checked the records and the Lodge is owned by a legal firm down in

Chicago. They hold the deed and pay the taxes and I
suppose that's owning it. So I phoned and got an
answering service. At one thirty in the afternoon I got
an answering service. And it took a while before they
told me it was an answering service. Now, just why
should a firm of lawyers be using an answering service
at that hour of the day? They wouldn't all of them be in
court. They wouldn't all of them be off on vacation, and
even if they were, there'd be at least one secretary to
take their calls.'

'Maybe,' I said, 'it is a one-man operation.'

The sheriff grunted. 'Doesn't sound like it. Jackson,
Smith, Dill, Hoen, and Ecklund. Took the answering
service gal half a minute to get it out of her mouth. She
sort of sang it. She had to sing it, I figured, or she'd
never make it. Say, where is Piper?'

'He had to go back to the university.'

'He didn't tell me he was going back.'

'He just failed to mention it,' I said. 'He'd known for
several days he had to go back today. Any reason he
shouldn't have?'

'No,' said the sheriff. 'I guess not. No doubt at all
what happened to Stefan. You wouldn't remember,
would you, what his last name was?'

'I never knew it,' I said.

'Well, so much for that,' the sheriff said. 'A little
embarrassing to have a corpse you don't know the name
of. Especially a man who had lived here as long as he
had. Stopped at the Lodge on my way up and there's
still no one there.'

The sheriff stayed for an hour or more. He acted like
a man who didn't want to go back to town, who hated
to get back to his office. We talked about the fishing,
and he said that some day he'd come out and fish
Killdeer Creek with me. We talked about grouse. I told
him I'd seen a fair amount of them. We talked about

the old days when people hunted ginseng in the hills and how you almost never found any ginseng now. Finally he got up and left.

I listened to the six o'clock radio news and again at ten and nothing was said about the Galloping Goose running into anything after it left Pine Bend. I went to bed after that, figuring that I wouldn't sleep, for I was still too excited, but I did. It had been a trying day and I was all worn out.

After breakfast I decided to go fishing. When I got to the bridge over Killdeer Creek a woman was standing on the bridge. I had taken a good look at the Lodge when I drove past and it still seemed to be deserted. But the woman was someone I had never seen before, and for no good reason I immediately figured she was someone from the Lodge. She was a blonde, a skinny sort of woman. She wore vivid yellow shorts and a skimpy yellow bra, but the bra seemed quite adequate, for she hadn't much to cover. Her hair was skinned back from her face and hung in a short ponytail down her back. She was leaning on the bridge railing, looking down into the pool. When I pulled the car over on the shoulder of the road just short of the bridge and got out, she turned her face toward me. The face was as skinny as her body. The structure of the jaw and cheekbones stood out beneath the skin, and the face had a sharp, almost pointed look.

'Is this where you found him?' she asked.

'I was not the one who found him,' I said, 'but, yes, this is where he was found. On the other side of the creek, just below the bridge.'

'Stefan was a fool,' she said.

'I didn't know the man,' I said. I thought it strange that she should speak as she did of him. After all, the man was dead.

'Were you a friend of his?' I asked.

'He had no friends,' she said. 'He had this silly hobby.'

'No hobby,' I said, 'is really silly if the hobbyist gets something out of it. I know a man who collects matchbook covers.' I didn't know anyone who collected matchbook covers. I just thought it was a good example of a rather pointless hobby.

'Did he have anything on him?' she asked. 'Anything in his pockets?'

It seemed a rather strange question for her to ask, but I answered her. 'Nothing,' I said. 'No identification. They don't know who he was.'

'Why, of course they do,' she said. 'They know he was Stefan. That's all we ever knew of him. That's all anyone needs to know.'

I heard footsteps behind me and swung around. A man was close behind me.

'Angela,' he said to the woman, 'you know you shouldn't be out here. What's the matter with you? Are you drunk again? You've been warned to leave the stuff alone.'

He said to me, 'Sorry if she's been bothering you.'

'Not at all,' I said. 'We've been talking. It's been most interesting.'

He was a bit shorter than I was, perhaps a little heavier, for he ran to chunkiness. His face ran to fullness and his hair was clipped short. He wore a checkered sports shirt and blue jeans, with heavy work shoes on his feet.

'We were talking about Stefan,' said the woman, and her voice carried the impression that she was embarrassing him and was glad of the chance to do so. 'About Stefan and his silly hobby.'

'But you are not interested in any hobbies he might have had,' said checkered shirt to me.

'Certainly I am,' I told him. 'I find it fascinating.'

'Come along,' he said to Angela. 'Back to the house with you.'

She came down off the bridge and stood beside him. She looked at me. 'I'll see you again,' she said.

'I hope so,' I told her. Before she had a chance to say any more he had taken her by the arm and turned her around and the two of them went marching down the road toward the Lodge. He didn't even say good-bye. He was a surly bastard.

There had been a lot going on between the two of them, I knew, that I had not understood. Most of it, I sensed, had to do with Stefan's hobby, and I wondered if the cubic photograph could have been the hobby. Thinking of it, I was fairly sure that my suspicion was correct. Angela had called his hobby silly, though, and it seemed to me that taking a photograph of Marathon was anything but silly.

There were a lot of things, I realised, I would have liked to talk with them about. When and how they'd gotten word of Stefan's death and when they'd gotten to the Lodge and how. Ordinarily when people came to the Lodge they flew into Pine Bend and Stefan took the Cadillac down to get them. Probably, I told myself, they'd hired someone to drive them up; after all, it didn't really matter. Come to think of it, no one really knew that Stefan had driven to Pine Bend to meet arrivals; we had just always assumed he had. I was a little disgusted with myself for wondering all those petty things; I was getting as nosy, I told myself, as Dora.

I lifted the rod out of the car and rigged it up, then got into my waders and went clumping down the embankment to the pool below the bridge.

I knew there were big trout in the pool, but I couldn't really put my heart into fishing. All the time that I was working at it, I was thinking of Stefan's body, stretched out on the bank across the stream. Every now and then I caught myself looking over my shoulder at the spot where he had been found. I got no strikes and no wonder, for I was too preoccupied with Stefan to pay attention to the fishing.

So I left the pool and went down the stream, walking in the shallow stretches, climbing out when I reached pools too deep for my waders. I left the scene of Stefan's death behind me and settled down to business. I hooked and landed one fair brookie in a stretch of rapid water at the head of a small pool, failed to set the hook when a big one, probably a rainbow, made a vicious lunge as the fly floated down the smooth water of a pool, edging in toward a cutbank where the big trout waited. I hauled in the line and made another cast to let the fly float in the self-same pattern, but there was no second strike. The big fellow that had made the strike might have felt the hook and was having none of it. I fished the pool thoroughly, but without a further strike. Several hundred feet beyond the pool I netted another brookie, perhaps a little bigger than the first one.

I climbed out on the bank and sat down on a rotting log, debating whether I should go on or quit. My fishing had not been too successful, but I had two fish, enough for supper, and there was that book on the Precambrian waiting at the cabin. I didn't want to quit. I wanted to keep on down the stream, not so much, perhaps, to keep on fishing as simply to stay out-of-doors, perhaps to stay away from the work that waited at the cabin. And, thinking that, I wondered rather seriously for the first time, I am sure, if I'd ever get the book done, whether I actually wanted to get it done. I had published little else and the department had excused the failure in light of knowing that I had the book, that I was working on it. I had been given the leave of absence to finish it, and I knew that I damn well better finish it. And yet I sat there, miserable, wondering if I'd ever finish it, knowing that through all the summer I'd use every excuse I could find not to work on it.

I thought of Neville's patch of lady's slippers and wondered if I should take the time to go and look for them. There was no reason that I should, of course, but I told myself that if I didn't see them now, in a few more days the blooms would be gone and I'd miss the seeing of them, for this year at least. But I made no move to go; I just stayed sitting there. I wasn't absolutely sure where the lady's slippers were, but from what Neville had said I didn't think I'd have much trouble finding them. Still I kept on sitting.

I've often wondered since what it was that kept me sitting on that rotten log. I could have continued with my fishing, I could have gone back to the car, I could have gone in search of Neville's lady's slippers. But I did none of these. And because I didn't, I now sit here writing this account when I should be working on my book.

Before I go any further, perhaps I should explain that Killdeer Creek lies deep in a wooded ravine between two steeply sloping hills. The bed of the creek lies in St Peter sandstone, but a slight distance up either hillside there are outcroppings of the Platteville limestone, although in large part these outcroppings may go quite unnoticed because in most instances they are masked by trees.

On the slope across the stream from me something was rustling around in the underlay of last autumn's leaves, and when I looked to see what was going on it took several seconds before I spotted the squirrel that was causing the commotion. He was nosing around, digging here and there, perhaps in hope of finding a nut left over from the autumn. He must somehow have sensed me watching, for suddenly he panicked and went scampering up the hillside. Veering to the right, he whipped into a small rock shelter. These tiny rock shelters are common in the hills, small areas of softer stone having eroded away and been capped by a layer of harder stone projecting out above them.

I sat quietly watching the shelter, and after a few

minutes the squirrel came sneaking out. He sat upright
and looked around, alert to any danger, then flashed up
the hill again. A few yards above the rock shelter he
crossed a small area of raw earth where the recent rains
apparently had washed away loose ground cover and
gouged into the underlying clay.

I followed his flight across the gouge and for a short
distance up the hill, then my mind caught up with me
and my eyes came back to focus on what they had seen,
but which had been delayed in its registration on my
brain. Protruding from that area of raw earth were not
one but two logs, or rather the ends of two logs. Above
the topmost log the ground apeared to have caved in,
leaving a small depression, and just above the depression
was another limestone outcropping.

I sat frozen, and my startled mind said no, that it was
all imagination. But hammering through my skull were
the words that Humphrey Highmore had spoken to me
only the day before: 'They cut logs to conceal the cave
mouth and shoveled dirt over the logs to conceal the
mine.'

You're stark, staring mad, I told myself; you're as bad
as Humphrey. But the idea still persisted, although I
tried to fight it down. A man simply did not sit down on a
rotting forest log and find a legendary mine.

To give myself something to do, I unshipped my rod,
dropped the reel into my pocket. Over the ages, I told
myself, a couple of trees could have fallen and been
covered by the slow accumulations of time. But the more
I looked at those two logs, the less it seemed that way.
Although I was too far away to see them, I found myself
believing I could discern the bite of ax strokes upon the
logs' protruding ends.

I crossed the stream and began clambering up the
slope. The going was slow, the hill so steep that I found
myself grabbing hold of saplings to help pull myself

forward. When I reached the small rock shelter into which the squirrel had popped, I paused to catch my breath. I saw that the shelter was somewhat larger than I had thought; a drift of dried autumn leaves had become lodged against the open face and made it seem smaller than it was. The floor of it was flat and a few feathers lay upon it; the floor was white with the chalkiness of old bird droppings. Perhaps I thought, it had been used for centuries as a sanctuary for ruffed grouse, or possibly by quail, although there were no longer very many quail. Toward the farther end of the shelter a small rock fall from the roof above seemed rather recent; in a few years, I told myself, other rock falls would occur and there'd no longer be a shelter. I felt sorry for the grouse, it was such a snug retreat for them against the night or weather.

Having gotten back my breath, I went on up the slope to where I'd seen the logs. Kneeling beside them, I knew I had found the mine. The wood was punky and wet from recent rains, but there could be no mistaking the still-existent evidence that they had been cut to a proper length by ax work. I could not quite believe my eyes and ran a hand across their cut ends for confirmation. And as I squatted there, stupidly running my hand back and forth over the wood, something ticked at me.

I went cold inside my guts and crouched hunched over, as if expecting someone or something to clout me on the head. There was nothing in the sound that was sinister; it was, in fact, a very gentle ticking, almost companionable – but this was not the place for it. And now there was no doubt at all that I had found the mine, for it had been a ticking that had driven the miners in terror from the hills.

I came to my feet and for a moment felt an illogical but powerful urge to go plunging down the hill, to put as much distance as possible between myself and this thing that ticked. The feeling didn't go away, but I stood against it and once I had managed to stand against it, it didn't seem quite so bad. I drove myself, literally drove myself, my feet not wanting to move but my brain making them move, the few feet up the slope to where the depression fell away above the logs. I could see that the depression extended deep into the ground, and I went down on my knees beside it. There seemed no bottom to it. I thrust my face down close above it and smelled the darkness and the coldness of another world. The cave, I knew, lay beneath my feet, and out of the opening into it came a wild, excited chittering of ticks.

'OK,' I said. 'OK, just take it easy. I'll be back to get you.'

I don't know why I said it. The words had come out of me without any conscious thought, as if some part of me of which I was not aware had grasped a situation I was unaware of and had answered for me, speaking to the thing that ticked and chittered as if it were a person.

I straightened, and even though the day was warm, I shivered. I would need a shovel, perhaps something that would play the part of a crowbar – the opening was too small and would have to be enlarged. And I would need, as well, a flashlight.

As I started to turn away, the ticking came again, a somewhat frantic and excited sound. 'It's all right,' I said. 'I'll be back. I promise.'

I was back in less than an hour. I had a shovel, a flashlight, my geologist's hammer, and a length of rope. I had not been able to find anything that resembled a crowbar, so I had brought along a pick that Neville and I had used when we had dug a trench to put in the footings for the cabin.

The thing inside the cave began ticking at me as I toiled up the slope, but now it sounded like a contented ticking, as if it knew I was coming back to get it. During the time that I had been gone, I'd had it out with myself on that score. You acted like a damn excited fool, I'd told myself. You allowed yourself to be stampeded into the acceptance of a fantasy situation that could not possibly exist. You can be excused for what you did in the un- thinking excitement of the moment; you acted under shock impact and were illogical. But you're illogical no longer. You've had time to think it over and now you know it's not a living thing down there in the cave, not a personality. Whatever is in there ticks, but it was ticking more than a century ago and it's unlikely that any living thing that was there more than a hundred years ago, and God knows how much longer ago than that, would still be there, alive and ticking. What you'll find will either be a mechanism of some sort or you'll find a perfectly natural explanation. And once having found it, you'll wonder why in hell you hadn't thought of it before.

I admit that while I had been talking so harshly to myself I hadn't examined that bit about finding a mechanism too closely. I had, I suspect, shied away from it because I didn't want to ask the question that would follow – what kind of mechanism, made by whom and for what purpose and how did it come to be there?

The thing to do, I told myself, was to rip out the logs, enlarge the opening, get down into the cave and find out what was going on. I was scared, of course. I had a right to be scared. I had thought of seeking out Humphrey (because Humphrey was the one man who had the right to be there), the sheriff, even that bastard at the Lodge. But I decided against it. I was surprised to find that I had become somewhat secretive about this business – afraid, perhaps, that it would come to nothing in the end and that I would become the laughingstock of the neighborhood.

So I got down to business. I shoveled away some dirt from around the logs, drove the pick between the logs and heaved. The bottom log came loose with less effort than I had expected, and I grabbed it with my hands and hauled it out. With the bottom log gone, the one on top of it was easily removed. Underneath the second log I could see another, but there was no need to bother with it, for with the two logs out, the way into the cave was open.

I shined the flashlight down into the cavity and saw that the floor was only about three feet down.

All the time that I had been working, the ticking had been going on, but I had paid little attention to it. I suppose I was getting somewhat accustomed to it. Or maybe I was consciously trying not to pay attention to it. Coming out of the dark maw of the cave, it was a spooky sound.

I let the shovel and the pick down into the cave, then, holding the flashlight, slid in myself. Once I hit the floor, I flashed the light into the cave's interior and was surprised to see it was rather small – ten feet wide or so and half again as deep, with the roof some three feet above my head. It was dry – there was very little overlay above it, and the slope was so steep that most of the water ran off without a chance to seep down into the cave.

I directed the light at the back of it and could see where the miners, more than a century ago, had done some digging. There were a couple of heaps of broken rock lying against the back wall of the cave, rocks that had been pried out of the rather thin-layered structure of the Platteville limestone.

The ticking came from the back of the cave. I stalked it step by cautious step. I could feel the short hairs at the back of my neck prickling but I kept on. I found it at the very back of the cave, protruding from one of the strata that had been broken by the miners. And, having found it, I sat flat upon my seat, keeping the light trained directly on it. Sitting there, with all the wind of courage drained out of me, I stared at it.

It really wasn't anything to be afraid of. It was not alive. It was, by rough definition, the mechanism I had told myself I'd find. It was cemented in the rock, only a part of it revealed.

It chittered at me and I said nothing back. If you'd paid me a million, I could have said nothing back.

Its end was a blunted point and seemed to be attached to some sort of cylinder. The cylinder, I estimated, was four inches or so in diameter. Above and all around it I could see the rough edges of the break that must have been made when the miners had worried off the forepart of the stone in which it was embedded.

And that was the hell of it – embedded!

The blunt end of the cylinder ticked at me.

'Oh, shut up,' I said. For not only was I frightened, I was exasperated. It was, I told myself, impossible. Someone, I thought, was pulling my leg, but for the life of me I couldn't figure who it might be or how they could have done it.

A rattle of falling rock and earth brought me around to face the entrance of the cave. I saw that someone stood there, but for a moment I couldn't make out who it was.

'What the hell do you mean,' I asked, 'sneaking up on me?'

'I'm sorry that I startled you,' the intruder said. 'Please believe me, I did not intend to do so. But it seems that you have found what we've been looking for.'

I thought I recognised the voice and now I saw who it was – the man who had come from the Lodge to get the woman he called Angela.

'Oh, it's you,' I said. I didn't try to conceal my dislike of him.

'Thornton,' he said, 'we have to make a deal. We must have what you have found.'

He came across the cave and stood above me. The cylinder made a few excited clicks, then fell silent.

He squatted down beside me. 'Let's have a look,' he said.

When I turned I had moved the flashlight. Now I brought it back to shine on the blunted nose of the cylinder.

'Have you got a name?' I asked.

'Sure. My name is Charles.'

'OK, Charles,' I said. 'You say you want this thing. As a start, perhaps, you can tell me what it is. And be damn careful what you tell me. For my part, I can tell you that it's embedded in the stone. See how the stone comes up close against it. No hole was ever bored to insert it. The limestone's wrapped around it. Do you have any idea what that means?'

He gulped, but didn't answer.

'I can tell you,' I said, 'and you won't believe it. This is Platteville limestone. It was formed at the bottom of an Ordovician sea at least four hundred million years ago, which means this thing is an artifact from at least as long ago. It fell into the sea, and when the limestone formed it was embedded in it. Now speak up and tell me what it is.'

He didn't answer me. He took a different tack. 'You know what we are,' he said.

'I have a good idea.'

'And you're not about to talk of it.'

'I think it most unlikely,' I said. 'To begin with, no one would believe me.'

'So there's no use in my pretending.'

'I rather doubt there is,' I said. 'You see, I have the saddle and Neville has the Marathon photograph.'

'The what kind of photograph?'

'The Marathon photograph. Marathon was a battle fought two and a half millennia ago. It fell from Stefan's pocket. Neville found it when he found the body.'

'So that is it,' he said.

'That is it, I said. 'and if you think you can come in here and demand this thing that I have found—'

'It's not a matter of demanding,' he assured me, 'nor of taking. We are beyond all demanding and all taking. We are civilised, you see.'

'Yeah,' I said. 'Civilised.'

'Look,' he said, almost pleading, 'there is no reason not to tell you. There were a people – you say four hundred million years ago, so I suppose it could have been that long ago . . .'

'A people?' I asked. 'What people? Four hundred million years ago there weren't any people.'

'Not here,' he said. 'Not on Earth. On another planet.'

'How would you know?' I asked.

'Because we found the planet.'

'We? You talk of we. Just who are "we"?'

'Myself. Angela. Stefan. Others like us. What is left of the human race. Stefan was different, though. Stefan was a throwback, a mistake.'

'You're jabbering,' I said. 'You don't make any sense. You're from up ahead, in the future, is that it?'

It was all insane, I told myself. Insane to ask that question. Asking as if it were just an ordinary thing, not to be greatly wondered at.

'Yes,' he said. 'A different world. You would not recognise it. Or the people in it.'

'I recognise you,' I said. 'You seem like anybody else. You're no different than anyone I know.'

He sighed, a patronising sigh. 'Think, Thornton,' he said. 'If you were to go back to a barbarian age, would you wear a jacket and a pair of slacks? Would you talk twentieth-century English? Would you—'

'No, of course not. I would wear a wolfskin and I'd learn – so that is it,' I said. 'Barbarian.'

'The term is relative,' he said. 'If I've offended you—'

'Not in the least,' I said. I had to be fair about it.

Depending on how far in time he had traveled, we might be barbarian. 'You were telling me about a planet you had found.'

'Burned out,' he said. 'The sun had novaed. All the water gone. The soil burned to powdered ash. You said half a billion years?'

'Almost that long,' I said.

'It could have been,' he said. 'The star is a white dwarf now. That would have been time enough. The planet had been inhabited by an intelligence. We found—'

'You mean you, personally? You saw this planet . . ?'

He shook his head. 'Not I. No one of my generation. Others. A thousand years ago.'

'In a thousand years,' I said, 'a lot could happen. . .'

'Yes, I know. Much is forgotten in a thousand years. But not this. We remember well; this is not a myth. You see, in all the time we've been out in space this is the first evidence of intelligence we found. There had been cities on that planet – well, maybe not cities, but structures. Nothing left, of course, but the stone that had been used in building them. It still was there, or most of it, stone on stone, much as it had been when it was laid. Some destruction, of course. Earthquakes, probably. No real weathering. Nothing left to cause weathering. All the water gone and the atmosphere as well. I forgot to say the atmosphere was gone.'

'Come to the point,' I said, rather brutally. 'This is all wonderful, of course. And very entertaining . . .'

'You don't believe me?'

'I can't be sure,' I said. 'But go on, anyhow.'

'You can imagine,' he said, 'how avidly and thoroughly our people examined the ruins of the structures. The work was, after a time, discouraging, for the ruins could tell us very little. Then, finally, a graven stone was found . . .'

'A graven stone?'

'A message stone. A slab of stone with a message carved upon it.'

'Don't tell me that you found this stone and then, right off, you read the message.'

'Not words,' he said. 'Not symbols. Pictures. You have a word. Funny pictures.'

'Cartoons,' I said.

'Cartoons. That is right. The cartoons told the story. The people of that planet knew their sun was about to nova. They had some space capability, but not enough to move a total population. What was worse, there was no planet they had ever found that could support their kind of life. I suspect it was much like our life, the same basis as our life. Oxygen and carbon. They didn't look like us. They were bugs. Many-legged, many-armed. Perhaps, in many ways, a more efficient organism than ourselves. They knew they were finished. Perhaps not all of them. They might have hoped they still could find a planet where a few of them could live. That way the germ plasma could be preserved, if they were lucky. The plasma, but not the civilisation, not their culture. Locating to another planet, having to come to grips with that planet and perhaps only a few of them to do it, they knew they would lose their culture, that it would be forgotten, that the few survivors could not maintain and preserve what they had achieved over many thousands of years. And it seemed important that at least the basics of their culture should be preserved, that it should not be lost to the rest of the galaxy. They were facing the prospect of cultural death. Do you have any idea of what the impact of cultural death might be like?'

'Like any other death,' I said. 'Death is death. Someone turns out the light.'

'Not quite,' he said. 'Not quite like any other death. No one likes the prospect of death. It may not be death itself, but the loss of identity we fear. The fear of being blotted out. Many men facing death are able to await it calmly because they feel they've made a good job out of life. They have done certain tasks or have stood for something they feel will cause them to be remembered. They are, you see, not losing identity entirely. They will be remembered, and that in itself is a matter of some identity. This is important for the individual; it is even more important for a race – a race proud of the culture it has built. Racial identity is even more important than individual identity. It is not too difficult for a man to accept the inevitability of his own death; it is almost impossible for him to accept the fact that some day there may be no humans, that the species will have disappeared.'

'I think I see,' I said. I had never thought of it before.

'So this race on the planet soon to be dead,' he said, 'took steps to preserve their culture. They broke it down to its basic concepts and essentials and they recorded it and put it into capsules. . . '

I started in surprise. 'You mean this?' I asked, gesturing at the cylinder enclosed within the stone.

'It is my hope,' he said, far too calmly, far too surely.

'You must be nuts,' I said. 'First for believing all this . . .'

'There were many capsules,' he said. 'There was a number indicated, but since we could not decipher their notation . . .'

'But they must have broadcast them. Simply flung them into space.'

He shook his head. 'They aimed them at suns. Given the kind of technology they had, many would have reached their destinations. They were gambling that one of them would come to earth on some distant planet and be picked up by some intelligence with enough curiosity and enough ingenuity . . .'

'They would have burned up when they entered the atmosphere.'

'Not necessarily. The technology . . .'

'Four hundred millions years ago,' I said. 'That long ago this precious planet of yours could have been across the galaxy from us.'

'We did not know, of course, how long ago,' he said, stubbornly, 'but from our calculations our sun and their sun would never have been impossibly far apart. They have matched galactic orbits.'

I squatted there and tried to think, and all I had was a roaring in the brain. It was impossible to believe, but there was the cylinder, embedded in the stone, a cylinder that ticked industriously to call attention to itself.

'The ticking,' said Charles, as if he knew my thoughts, 'is something we had never thought of. Perhaps it's activiated when anything fulfilling certain biological requirements comes within a certain distance of it. But, then, of course, we never expected to stumble upon one of the capsules.'

'What did you expect, then?' I asked. 'From what you've said, you have been hunting for a capsule.'

'Not really hunting for one,' he told me. 'Just hoping we'd find some evidence that some time in the past one had been found. Either found and destroyed or lost – maybe found and at least a portion of its message extracted from it, extracted perhaps, then lost again because it did not fit in with human thought. Always hoping, of course, that we might find one tucked away in some obscure hiding place, in a small museum, maybe, in an attic or a storeroom of an ancient house, in some old temple ruin.'

'But why come back into the past, why come here? Surely in your own time—'

'You do not understand,' he said. 'In our time there is very little left. Very little of the past. The past does not last forever – either materially or intellectually. The intellectual past is twisted and distorted; the material past, the records and the ruins of it, are destroyed or lost or decay away. And if by "here" you mean in this particular place and time, we do few operations here. The Lodge – I understand that is what you call it – is what in your time you might term a rest and recreation area.'

'But the years you've spent at it,' I said. 'All these years in a search that had so little chance.'

'There is more to it than that,' he said. 'The finding of an alien capsule, how would you say it in the idiom of today? The finding of an capsule is the big prize on the board. It was something we were always on the lookout for, our investigative sense was always tuned to some hint that one might exist or at one time had existed. But we did not spend all our time—'

'Investigative? You said investigative. Just what the hell are you investigating?'

'History,' he said. 'Human history. I thought there was no question that you would have guessed it.'

'I am stupid,' I said. 'I didn't guess it. You must have shelves of history. All you have to do is read it.'

'As I told you, there's not much of the past left. When there are nuclear wars and a large part of the planet goes back to barbarism, the past goes down the drain. And what little there is left becomes very hard to find.'

'So there will be nuclear wars,' I said. 'We had begun to hope that Earth might never have to face that. Could you tell me—'

'No,' said Charles, 'I can't.'

We hunkered there, the two of us, looking at the capsule.

'You want it?' I asked.

He nodded.

'If we can get it out undamaged,' I said.

The capsule clucked quietly at us, companionably.

I pulled the rock hammer out of my belt.

'Here,' I said, handing him the flashlight.

He took it and held it with its light trained on the capsule while I leaned close and studied the rock.

'We might be in luck,' I said. 'There is a bedding plane, a seam, running just below the capsule. Limestone's funny stuff. The layers can be either thick or thin. Sometimes it peels, sometimes it has to be broken.'

I tapped the bedding plane with the hammer. The stone flaked under the blows. Turning the hammer around to use the chisel end, I pecked away at the seam.

'Hand me the pick,' I said, and he handed it to me.

I had little room to work in, but I managed to drive the sharp end of the pick deep into the seam and a layer of the limestone peeled away and fell. The capsule was exposed along its lower side, and it took only a little more juidicious chipping away of the rock to free it. It was some eighteen inches long and heavier than I had imagined it would be.

Charles put the flashlight down on the floor of the cave and reached out his hands for it.

'Not so fast,' I said. 'We have a deal to make.'

'You can keep the saddle.'

'I already have it,' I said. 'I intend to keep it.'

'We'll repair it for you. We'll even exchange a new one for it. We'll teach you how to use it.'

'I don't think so,' I said. 'I'm satisfied right here. I know how to get along right here. Seems to me a man could get into a lot of trouble taking off to other times. Now if you had some more photographs like the Marathon photograph. . . Say a couple of hundred of them, of selected subjects.'

He put his hands up to his head in anguish.

'But we don't,' he said. 'We never take such photographs.'

'Stefan took them.'

He choked in frustration. 'How can I make you understand! Stefan was a freak, a throwback. He got kicks out of violence, out of blood. That's why we kept him here. That was why he was never allowed to go out in the field.

He sneaked out whenever he could and took what you call the photographs. There is a name for them. . . '

'Holographs,' I said.

'I guess that's the word. A mechanism using the laser principle. It was a mistake to put him on our team. It meant we had to cover up for him. We couldn't report or admit what he was doing. We had to consider the honor of the team. We talked with him, we pleaded with him, but he was beyond all shame. He was a psychopath. How he ever succeeded in covering up his condition so he could be appointed to the team—'

'Psychopaths,' I said, 'are tricky.'

He pleaded with me, 'Now you understand?'

'Not too well,' I said. 'You stand aghast at violence, You are turned off by blood. And yet you study history and, more often than not, history turns on violence. It can be a bloody business.'

He shuddered. 'We find enough of it. We are repelled by it, but it's sometimes necessary to consider it. We do not enjoy it: Stefan did enjoy it. He knew how we felt about it. He hid away his photographs, afraid we would destroy them. We would have if we'd found them.'

'You hunted for them,' I said.

'Everywhere. We never found their hiding place.'

'So there are some around?'

'I suppose there are. But if you think they can be found, forget it. You said psychopaths are tricky.'

'Yes, I guess I did,' I said. 'In such a case, there can't be any deal.'

'You mean you'll keep the capsule?'

I nodded and tucked it underneath my arm.

'But why?' he shouted. 'Why?'

'If it's valuable to you,' I told him, 'it should be valuable to us.'

And I thought to myself, what in the name of Holy Christ am I doing here, hunkered down in a cave that was an olden mine, arguing with a man out of the human future about a silly cylinder out of the nonhuman past?

'You would have no way to come by the information that the capsule carries,' he said.

'How about yourself? How about your people?'

'They'd have a better chance. We can't be entirely sure, of course, but we'd have a better chance.'

'I suppose,' I said, 'that you expect to find some nonhuman knowledge, a cultural concept based on nonhuman values. You expect a lot of new ideas, a windfall of new concepts, some of which could be grafted on your culture, some of which could not.'

'That's the whole point, Thornton. Even if you could extract the knowledge, how would your age put it to use? Don't forget that some of it, perhaps much of it, might run counter to your present concepts. What if it said that human rights must take precedence, both in theory and in practice, over property rights? In practice as well as in theory – right now, of course, human rights do in certain aspects take precedence in theory, even in law, but how about in practice? What if you found something that condemned nationalism and gave a formula for its being done away with? What if it proved patriotism were so much utter hogwash? Not that we can expect the contents of this capsule to deal with such things as human rights and nationalism. The information in this capsule, I would suspect, will include a lot of things we've never even thought of. How do you think the present day, your present day, would take to such divergence from what you consider as the norm? I can tell you. It would be disregarded, it would be swept beneath the rug, it would be laughed and sneered to nothing. You might as well smash this capsule into bits as give it to your people.'

'How about yourselves?' I asked. 'How can you be sure you'll put it to good use?'

'We have to,' he said. 'If you saw Earth as it is up in

my time, you would know we'd have to. Sure, we can travel out in space. We can travel into time. But with all these things, we still are hanging on by our fingernails. We'll use it; we'll use anything at all to keep the human race in business. We are the end product of thousands of years of mismanagement and bungling – your mismanagement and bungling. Why do you think we spend our lives in coming back to study history? For the fun of it? The adventure? No, I tell you, no. We do it to find where and how the human race went wrong, hoping to glean some insight into how it might have gone right, but didn't. To find an old lost knowledge that might be put to better use than you ever put it to. We are the lost race digging through the garbage of men who lived before us.'

'You're sniveling,' I said. 'You are feeling sorry for yourself.'

'I suppose so,' he said. 'I'm sorry. We no longer are the frozen-faced realists of this time, afraid of emotion, any more than you are the rough, tough barbarian you'd meet if you went back a couple of thousand years. The human race has changed. We are the ones who were stripped naked. We decided long ago we could no longer afford the luxury of violence, of cutthroat economic competition, of national pride. We are not the same people you know. I don't say we are better, only different and with different viewpoints. If we want to weep, we weep; if we want to sing, we sing.'

I didn't say anything; I just kept looking at him.

'And if you keep the capsule,' he asked, 'what will you do with it, you personally, not your culture? To whom would you give it, whom would you tell about it? Who would listen to your explanation? Could you survive the scarcely hidden disbelief and laughter? How could you, once you'd told your story, the story I have told you – how could you face your colleagues and your students?'

'I guess I couldn't,' I said. 'Here, take the goddamn thing.'

He reached out and took it. 'I thank you very much,' he said. 'You have earned our gratitude.'

I felt all cut up inside. I wasn't sure of anything. To have something in one's hand, I thought, that might change the world, then give it away, be forced to give it away because I knew that in my time it would not be used, that there could be no hope that it would be used – that was tough to take. I might have felt different about it, I knew, if I could have given the cylinder to someone else than this little twerp. I didn't know why I disliked him; I had never even asked myself what there was to dislike about him. Then, suddenly, I knew; it all came to me. I disliked him because there were too many centuries between us. He was still a human, sure, but not the same kind of human as I was. Time had made a difference between us. I had no idea of how many years there might be between us – I hadn't even asked him, and I wondered why I hadn't. Times change and people change, and those cumulative changes had made us different kinds of humans.

'If you'll come up to the house,' he said, 'I could find a drink.'

'Go to hell,' I said.

He started to leave, then turned back to me. 'I hate to leave like this,' he said. 'I know how you must feel. You don't like me, I am sure, and I can't with all honesty say I care too much for you. But you have done a great, although unwitting, service for us, and I have a deep sense of gratitude. Aside from all of that, we are two human beings. Please don't shame me, Thornton. Please accord me the luxury of being decent to you.'

I grunted boorishly at him, but I got up, picked up the tools and followed after him.

When we came into the Lodge, Angela was slumped in

a chair. A whiskey bottle stood on the table beside her.
She struggled to her feet and waved a half-filled glass at
me, spilling liquor on the rug.

'You must not mind her,' Charles said to me. 'She is
compensating.'

'And who the hell wouldn't compensate?' she asked.
'After months of tracking down and keeping up with
Villon in the stews of fifteenth-century Paris . . .'

'Villon,' I said, not quite making it a question.

'Yes, François Villon. You have heard of him?'

'Yes,' I said. 'I have heard of him. But why . . .'

She gestured at Charles. 'Ask the mastermind,' she
said. 'He's the one who figures it all out. A man out of his
time, he said. Find this Villon, a man out of his time. A
genius when there were few geniuses. Pluck wisdom from
him. Find out who he really was. And so I found him and
he was just a filthy poet, a burglar, a chaser after women,
a brawler, a jailbird.' She said to me, 'The past human
race was a bunch of slimy bastards, and the people of
your time are no better than the others that have come
before you. You're all a bunch of slimy bastards.'

'Angela,' Charles said, sharply, 'Mr Thornton is our
guest.'

She swung on him. 'And you,' she said, 'while I'm
wading through the stench and depravity and obscenity
of medieval Paris, where are you? In a little monastery
library somewhere in the Balkans, feeling sanctimonious
and holy, and no doubt somewhat supercilious, pawing
through parchments, searching on slimmest rumor for
evidence of something that you damn well know never
did exist.'

'But, my dear,' he said, 'it does exist.'

He put the cylinder on the table beside the whiskey
bottle.

She stared at it, swaying a little. 'So you finally found
it, you little son of a bitch,' she said. 'Now you can go

home and lord it over everyone. You can live out your life as the little creep who finally found a capsule. There's one good thing about it – the team will be rid of you.'

'Shut up,' said Charles. 'I didn't find it. Mr Thornton found it.'

She looked at me. 'How come you knew about it?' she asked.

'I told him about it,' said Charles.

'Oh, great,' she said. 'So now he knows about us.'

'He did, anyhow,' said Charles. 'So, I suspect, does Mr Piper. They found one of Stefan's cubes, and when the plane hit Stefan's parked saddle, it fell in Mr Thornton's yard. These men aren't stupid, dear.'

I told him, 'It is good of you to say so.'

'And the sheriff, too,' she said. 'The two of them and the sheriff came snooping yesterday.'

'I don't think the sheriff knows,' I said. 'The sheriff doesn't know about the saddle or the cube. All he saw was that contraption over there. He thought it might be a game of some sort.'

'But you know it's not a game.'

'I don't know what it is,' I said.

'It's a map,' said Charles. 'It shows when and where we are.'

'All the others can look at it,' said Angela, 'or another like it and know where all the others are.'

She pointed. 'That is us down there,' she said.

It made no sense to me. I could see why they'd need a map like that, but not how it could work.

She moved closer to me and took me by the hand. 'Look down, she said. 'Look down into the center of it. Let's move closer to it and look down into the center of it.'

'Angela,' warned Charles, 'you know that's not allowed.'

'For the love of Christ,' she said, 'he has something

coming to him. He found that stinking cylinder and gave
it to you.'

'Look,' I said, 'whatever is going on, leave me out of
it.' I tried to pull my hand away, but she hung on to it,
her nails cutting into my flesh.

'You're drunk,' said Charles. 'You are drunk again.
You don't know what you're doing.' There was something in his voice that told me he was afraid of her.

'Sure, I'm drunk,' she said, 'but not all that drunk.
Just drunk enough to be a little human. Just drunk
enough to be a little decent.'

'Down,' she said to me. 'Look down into the center of
it.' And I did, God help me, look down into the center of
that weird contraption. I guess I must have thought that
looking down into it might humor her and end the situation. That's just a guess, however; I don't honestly
remember for what reason, if I had a reason, I looked
down into it. Later on – but the point is that it was later
on and not at that particular moment – I did some
wondering if she might have been a witch, then asked
myself what a witch might he, and got so tangled up in
trying to figure out a definition that it all came to
nothing.

But, anyhow, I looked down and there was nothing I
could see except a lot of swirling mist – the mist was dark
instead of white. There was something about it that I
didn't like, a certain frightfulness to it, and I went to step
away, but before I could take the step the dark mist
inside the cubicle seemed to expand rapidly and engulf
me.

The world went away from me and I was a consciousness inside a blackness that seemed to hold neither
time nor space, a medium that was suspended in a
nothingness in which there was no room for anything or
anyone but the consciousness – not the body, but the
consciousness – of myself and Angela.

For she still was with me in that black nothingness and I still could feel her hand in mine, although even as I felt the pressure of her hand I told myself it could not be her hand, for in this place neither of us had hands; there was no place or room for hands. Once I had said that to myself, I realised that it was not her hand that I seemed to feel so much as the presence of her, the essence of her being, which seemed to be coalescing with my being as if we had ceased to be two personalities, but had in some strange way become a single personality, although not so much a part of one another as to have lost our identities.

I felt a scream rising in my throat, but I had no throat and I had no mouth and there was no way to scream. I wondered, in something close to terror, what had happened to my body and if I'd ever get it back. As I tried to scream I sensed Angela moving closer, as if she might be extending comfort. And there was comfort, certainly, in knowing she was there. I don't think she spoke to me or actually did anything at all, but I seemed to realise somehow that there were just the two of us in this great nothingness and that there was no room for more than just the two of us; that here there was no place for fear or even for surprise.

Then the dark nothingness drained away, but the draining did not give us back our bodies. We still were disembodied beings, hanging for a moment over a nightmare landscape that was bleak and dark, a barren plain that swept away to jagged mountains notched against the sky. We hung there for a moment only, not really long enough to see where we were – as if a picture had been flashed upon a screen, then suddenly cut off. A glimpse was all I had.

Then we were back in the empty nothingness and Angela had her arms around me – all of her around me – and it was very strange, for she had no arms or body and neither did I, but it seemed to make no difference. The touch of her was comforting, as it had been before, but this time more than comforting, and in that nothingness my soul and mind and the memory of my body cried out to her as another human being and another life. Instinctively, I reached out for her – and reached out within everything I had or had ever had until the semblance of what we once had been intertwined and meshed and we melted into one another. Our beings came together, our minds, our souls, our bodies. In that moment we knew one another in a way that would have been impossible under other circumstances. We crawled into one another until there were not two of us, but one. It was sexual, in part, but far more than sexual. It was the kind of experience that is sought in a sexual embrace but never quite achieved. It was complete fulfillment and it did not subside. It reached a high and stayed there. It was an ectasy that kept on and on, and it could have gone on forever, I suppose, if it had not been for that one little dirty corner of my busy brain that somehow stood aside and wondered how it might have been with someone other than a bitch like Angela.

That did it. The magic went away. The nothingness went away. We were back in the Lodge, standing beside the strange contraption. We still were holding hands, and she dropped my hand and turned to face me. Her face was white with fury, her voice cold.

'Remember this,' she said. 'No woman will ever be quite the same again.'

Charles, still standing where he had been before, picked up the nearly empty whiskey bottle. He laughed, a knowing and insulting laugh. 'I promised you a drink,' he said. 'You probably need one now.'

'Yes, you did,' I said. I started across the room toward him, and he picked up the glass that Angela had been using and began to pour the drink. 'We are short of glasses, he said. 'Under the circumstances, I don't imagine you will mind.'

I let him have it, squarely in the face. He was not expecting it, and when he saw the fist coming in it was too late for him to duck. I caught him in the mouth and he went back and down as if he had been sledged. The glass and bottle fell from his hands and rolled across the carpeting, both of them spewing whiskey.

I felt good about belting him. I had wanted to do it ever since I saw him for the first time that morning. Thinking that, I was aghast that so little time had passed.

He didn't try to get up. Maybe he couldn't; maybe he was out. For all I cared he might as well be dead.

I turned and walked toward the door. As I opened it, I looked back. Angela was standing where I'd left her, and she didn't stir when I looked at her. I tried to think of something I should say to her, but nothing came to mind. I suspect it was just as well.

My car was standing in the driveway and the sun was far down the western sky. I took a deep breath – I suppose, unconsciously, I was trying to wipe away any clinging odor of the fog of nothingness, although, to tell the truth, I had never noticed any odor.

When I got into the car and put my hands on the wheel, I noticed that the knuckles of my right hand were bleeding. When I wiped the blood off on my shirt, I could see the toothmarks.

Back at the cabin I parked the car and, climbing to the porch, sat down in a chair. I didn't do a thing, just stayed sitting there. The Galloping Goose came over, heading south. Robins scratched in the leaves underneath the brush beyond our patch of lawn. A sparrow sang as the sun went down.

When it was dark and the lightning bugs came out, I went indoors and made myself some supper. After I had eaten I went out on the porch again, and now I found that I could think a bit, although the thinking made no sense.

The thing that stuck closest to my mind was that brief glimpse I'd gotten of the bleak, dark landscape. It had only been a glimpse, a flashing on and off, but it must have been impressed deeply on my brain. For I found that there were details I had not been aware of, that I would have sworn I had never seen. The plain had seemed level in its blackness, but now I could recall that it was not entirely level, that there were mounds upon it and here and there jagged spears extending upward that could be nothing else than the stumps of shattered masonry. And I knew as well, or seemed to know, that the blackness of the plain was the blackness of molten rock, frozen forever as a monument of that time when the soil and rock beneath had bubbled in a sudden fire.

It was the future, I was certain, that Angela had shown me, the future from which she and the other scavengers had come, probing back across unknown centuries to find out not only what their far forebears had known, but as well those things they might have uncovered or discovered, but had not really known. Although I wondered, as I thought of it, what could possibly have been the so-far-unrecognised significance of a man like Villon? A poet, sure, an accomplished medieval poet who had a modern flair and flavour, but as well a thief and a vagabond who must at many times have felt the shadow of the hangman's noose brush against his neck.

What had we missed in Villon, I wondered, what might we have missed in many other events and men? What could be the significance that we had missed and which had been recognised and now was sought by our far descendants in that black and frozen world up ahead of us? Sought by those who now came back among us to sift through the dustbins of our history, seeking what we unknowingly might have thrown away.

If we could only talk with them, I thought, if only they

would talk with us – and even as I thought it, I knew how impossible it was. There was about them a supercilious quality that would not allow them to, that we would never stand for in that it scarcely masked the contempt that they felt for us. It would be akin to a radio astronomer going back to ancient Babylon to talk with a priest-astronomer. In both cases, I knew, the gulf would not be only one of knowledge but of attitude.

A faithful whippoorwill that clocked in every evening shortly after dusk began his haunted chugging. Listening to it, I sat and let the woodland peace creep in. I'd forget it all, I told myself, I'd wipe it from my mind – I had a book to write. There was no purpose and no need to fret about something that would not happen for God knows how many millennia from now.

I knew, of course, that I was wrong. This was not something that could be forgotten. Too much had happened, too much remained unsaid for the incident to be ignored. There probably was, as well, too much at stake, although when I tried to sort out what specifically might be at stake, I had no luck at all. There were questions that needed answering, explanations to be given, a fuller story to be told. And there was just one place to get those questions answered.

I went down off the porch and got into the car. The Lodge was dark when I pulled into the driveway. There was no answer to my knock; when I tried the latch the door came open. I stepped inside and stood in the dark, not calling out. I think I knew there was no one there. My eyes became somewhat accustomed to the dark. Moving cautiously, alert to chairs that might trip me up, I went into the room. My foot crunched on something and I stopped in midstride. Then I saw it – the shattered wreckage of the time-map. I found a pack of matches in my pocket and struck one of them. In the brief flaring of its light I saw that the cubicle had been smashed.

Someone, I guessed, had taken a maul, or perhaps a rock to it.

The match burned down and I shook it out. I turned about and left, shutting the door behind me. And now, I thought, the people of the hills would have another mystery about which to speculate. There was the shattered time-map, of course, which when it was found would be a topic of conversation for a year or more at most. The real mystery, however, would be the question of what had happened to the people of the Lodge – the story of how one summer they had disappeared, leaving the Cadillac standing in the garage, and had not come back again. The unpaid taxes would pile up, and at some time in the future someone might pay up the taxes and get title to the place, but that would make no difference to the legend. Through many years to come the story would be told at the Trading Post, and given time the Lodge might become a haunted house and thus the story would be ensured a special kind of immortality.

Back at the cabin, with the fireflies winking in the woods and the faithful whippoorwill chunking from across the hollow, I tried to console myself by thinking I had done everything that a man could do, although I had the horrid feeling I had failed. And I realised, as well, that now I had lost any chance I might have to do anything at all. This, then, had to be the end of it. The best thing for me, I told myself, was to get back to the book in the hope that as I worked I might forget – or, if not forget, ease the sharpness of the memory.

I tried. For three whole days I tried. I drove myself and got some writing done. When I read it over, I tore it up and wrote it once again. The second draft was no better than the first.

While I sat working at the kitchen table I could feel the saddle in the closet sneaking up on me. I took it out of the closet and, dragging it down the hill, chucked it in a deep ravine. It didn't help; it still sneaked up on me. So I went down into the ravine and retrieved it, throwing it back into the closet.

Running out of groceries, I went to the Trading Post. Humphrey was sitting outside the door, his chair tipped back against the building. I picked up the groceries and a letter for Neville. I sat an hour or two with Humphrey while he talked about the mine. I let him do the talking; I was afraid to say anything for fear I'd make a conversational slip and tip him off to what I knew about it.

The letter from Neville was short, written by a man who was in a hurry. He was off for Greece, he wrote – 'I need to see Marathon again.'

Returning home with the groceries, I bundled up the notes and drafts I had been working on and jammed them in the briefcase, then went fishing. Fishing helped, I think. If I could have gone on fishing, it would have been all right. If I could have spent the summer fishing, I might have worked it out. But the fishing didn't last long.

I had picked up three fairly good trout by the time I reached the place from which, sitting on a log, I had spotted the protruding log ends that had led me to the mine.

Standing in the stream and looking up the hill, I could see the entrance to the mine, and a short distance below it the rock shelter into which the squirrel had dived.

Then my mind played a sneaky trick on me. Looking at the rock shelter, the thought struck me – that hidden, obscure bit of evidence that had been lying in the back part of my mind, unnoticed until now. I have often wondered since why it could not have passed me by, why it would not have remained hidden, why the computer in my brain felt compelled to haul it forth.

When I had glanced into the shelter, I recalled, I had seen the drifting feathers and the chalky droppings of the birds that had used it for a shelter, while toward the farther end there had been a small rockfall. And it was something about this rockfall that my mind had pounced upon – something that at the time I must subconsciously have noted, but which my brain, in the excitement of the moment, had tucked away for consideration later.

Now, suddenly, it brought forward for consideration the fact that while the roof of the shelter had been limestone, the rockfall had not been limestone, but green shale instead. Green shale, the kind of stone that could by picked from this very stream bed, chunks of soft, smooth rock eroded from the Decorah beds that lay atop the Platteville. The shale could not have been the product of the rockfall; it had been carried there.

Incredible as it may seem, I believe that in that moment I sensed exactly what had happened – an incredible hypothesis rising full-blown out of an incredible situation.

I rebelled against it. To hell with it, I thought; I have had enough; I don't need any more. But even so, I knew I had to have a look; I would never rest until I'd had a look. Not knowing would haunt me. I hoped, I think (it's hard to remember now), that I would find the fall was limestone and not shale at all.

When I went to look, I found my subconscious had been right. The rock was shale, worn smooth by water action. And underneath the little pile of rocks were hidden two of Stefan's photographic cubes.

I squatted there and looked at them, remembering back to what Charles had said. A psychopath, he'd said. A psychopath and he did this filthy thing, then hid the cubes away so we couldn't find them.

Strangely, I couldn't be absolutely sure of the words he had used. Had he said psychopath? Had filthy been the word he had used, or some other word that was very much like it? I remembered he had said violence, but realised he had meant something more than violence, something perhaps so subtle that he could not explain it to me in terms I would understand. And that was the crux of it, of course, illustrative of the gulf between his time and mine.

I tried to imagine a twentieth-century social worker attempting to explain compassion for the poor to an aristocrat of Rome who only thought in terms of bread and circuses, then knew the analogy was a bad one, for the gulf of understanding between the social worker and the Roman would have been narrow compared to the gulf between myself and Charles.

So here, this day, I sit at the kitchen table, nearly done with writing, with the two cubes beside the pile of paper. I wonder at the blind course of circumstance that could have led me to them. And I wonder, too, rather bitterly, about the burden of knowledge that one man must carry, knowing it is true and yet unable to speak a word of it, condemned to write of it in secret for his own salvation (and I'm beginning to think it is no salvation).

I wonder, as well, why I cannot feel compassion for these people of the future, why I cannot see them as our descendants, children of our children many times removed. Why I cannot wish them well. But, no matter what I do, I can't. As if they were alien, as alien as that other people who had broadcast cylinders to the stars — aliens in time rather than space.

Now about the cubes.

One of them, I am fairly certain, although I cannot be entirely sure since I'm no historian, contains a photo of that moment on Christmas Day in the Year of Our Lord 800 when Charlemagne was crowned by Leo III as emperor of the West. Charlemange (if it indeed is he) is a thug, a massive brute that one dislikes instinctively, while Leo is a fussy little person who seems more overwhelmed by the situation than is Charlemagne.

I cannot be sure, of course, but a number of things

make me believe the photo is of Charlemagne and Leo, not the least of which is that this would be, in historic context, the one coronation that a man going into time would want to photograph. Or, rather, perhaps the coronation a man of my own time would want to photograph. I realise that with Stefan there can be no telling. If his thinking and his viewpoint were as twisted as the viewpoint of the others of his time, God knows what his reasons might have been for doing anything at all. Although he did photograph Marathon – and the thought occurs to me that his doing so may mean he did think somewhat along the lines we do and may possibly supply a clue to his so-called pschosis. Could the fact that he was believed psychotic by the people of his time mean no more than that he was a throwback?

I find small comfort in the thought. I would prefer to think he was not a throwback. Knowing he was not, I could feel more comfortable about the remaining cube.

I wish now I had taken the time to know Stefan better; as it stands, no one really knew him. He had been around for years, and all we ever did was wave at him as we went driving past. He was a difficult man, of course. Humphrey said he was the sort of man who would not even tell his name. But we, all of us, could have made a greater effort than we did.

Sitting here, I try to reconstruct him. I try to envision his sneaking down the hollow to hide his cubes. He must have been on the way to cache the Marathon cube when he met his death. Illogical as it may seem, I have even wondered if he was engaged in some ghastly joke, if he had deliberately planted an intentional clue by being killed just below the bridge to enable me, or someone else, to find the hidden cubes. Could there have been two authentic and historic cubes that were intended to lend some credence to the third? This is all insane, of course, but under stressful circumstances a man thinks insanity.

My own thinking must be going faulty; I am clutching at any evidence that will enable me to discount the third cube.

The photograph shows a crucifixion. The cross is not a tall one; the feet of the man upon it are no more than two feet or so above the ground. The wrists are nailed to the crossbar, but the ankles are tied to the post, with no support for the feet. To support the body so that the nails will not tear out, a wooden peg had been passed beneath the crotch and driven in the post. In the distance lies an ancient city. Half a dozen bored and listless soldiers – I take them to be Roman soldiers – lounge about, leaning on their spears, there apparently to prevent interference with the execution. Besides the soldiers there are only a few others, a small band of silent men and women who simply stand and watch. A dog sniffing at the post and one knows, instinctively, that in a little while he'll lift his leg against it.

There is no mocking placard nailed upon the cross. There is no crown of thorns. There are no other crosses, bearing thieves, to flank the single cross. There is no sign of glory.

And yet – and yet – and yet . . . Stefan filmed a moment out of Marathon, snatched for posterity the significance of that far-gone Christmas day, proving that indeed he had a keen sense of the historical as it might be interpreted by the culture of the present. The present, not the future. If he had been so right about the other two, could he have been wrong about the third? There had been, of course, many crucifixions, the punishment reserved for slaves, for thieves, for the contemptibles. But of all of them, in the context of history, only one stands out. Could Stefan have missed that one? Much as I might like to think so, I do not believe he did.

The thing that saddens me, that leaves in me a feeling of chilling emptiness, is that nothing of importance seems to be transpiring. There is the sense of shoddy death (if death can be shoddy, and I think it often is). Here the soldiers wait for the dying to be done, so they can be off to better things. The others simply wait, with resignation on their faces; there is nothing one can do against the power of Rome.

And yet, I tell myself, if this is the way it really was, this is the way it should have stayed, this is the way the event should have been transmitted to us. Out of this sad and empty happening, Christianity might have built a greater strength than it has from all the trappings of imagined glory.

The head of the victim on the cross had fallen forward, with the chin resting on the chest. Turn the cube as I may, I cannot not see the face.

If I could look upon the face, I think I would know. Not by recognising the face, for we do not know the face – all we have is the imaginings of long-dead artists, not all of them agreeing. But from some expression on the face, from something in the eyes.

I wonder about the saddle. Could it somehow be fixed? Could it be made to function once again? Could I figure out, from scratch, how to operate it?

(Editor's note: This manuscript was found in the briefcase of Andrew Thornton, along with the notes for a book he had been writing, after Thornton's disappearance. Police theorise he may have wandered off and been killed by a bear in some densely wooded and remote area where there would be little hope of finding his body. The possibility he may have wandered off is supported by his distraught frame of mind, which the manuscript reveals. Thornton's disappearance was reported by his close friend, Neville Piper, upon his return from Greece. The saddle mentioned in the manuscript has not been found; there is some question it existed.

Neither have the cubes been found. Dr Piper, who presently is engaged in writing a book on the Battle of Marathon, setting forth some new findings, disclaims any knowledge of the so-called Marathon Photograph.)

The Grotto Of The Dancing Deer

Luis was playing his pipe when Boyd climbed the steep path that led up to the cave. There was no need to visit the cave again; all the work was done, mapping, measuring, photographing, extracting all possible infor- mation from the site. Not only the paintings, although the paintings were the important part of it. Also there had been the animal bones, charred and the still remain- ing charcoal of the fire in which they had been charred; the small store of natural earths from which the pigments used by the painters had been compounded – a cache of valuable components, perhaps hidden by an artist who, for some reason that could not now be guessed, had been unable to use them; the atrophied human hand, severed at the wrist (why had it been severed and, once severed, left there to be found by men thirty millennia removed?); the lamp formed out a chunk of sandstone, hollowed to accommodate a wad of moss, the hollow filled with fat, the moss serving as a wick to give light to those who painted. All these and many other things, Boyd thought with some satisfaction; Gavarnie had turned out to be, possibly because of the sophisticated scientific methods of investigation that had been brought to bear, the most significant cave painting site ever studied – perhaps not as spectacular, in some ways, as Lascaux, but far more productive in the data obtained.

No need to visit the cave again, and yet there was a reason – the nagging feeling that he had passed something up, that in the rush and his concentration on the other work, he had forgotten something. It had made small impression on him at the time, but now, thinking back on it, he was becoming more and more inclined to believe it might have importance. The whole thing probably was a product of his imagination, he told himself. Once he saw it again (if, indeed, he could find it again, if it were not a product of retrospective worry), it might prove to be nothing at all, simply an impression that had popped up to nag him.

So here he was again, climbing the steep path, geologist's hammer swinging at his belt, large flashlight clutched in hand, listening to the piping of Luis who perched on a small terrace, just below the mouth of the cave, a post he had occupied through all the time the work was going on. Luis had camped there in his tent through all kinds of weather, cooking on a camper's stove, serving as self-appointed watch-dog, on alert against intruders, although there had been few intruders other than the occasional curious tourist who had heard of the project and tramped miles out of the way to see it. The villagers in the valley below had been no trouble; they couldn't have cared less about what was happening on the slope above them.

Luis was no stranger to Boyd; ten years before, he had shown up at the rock shelter project some fifty miles distant and there had stayed through two seasons of digging. The rock shelter had not proved as productive as Boyd initially had hoped, although it had shed some new light on the Azilian culture, the tag-end of the great Western European prehistoric groups. Taken on as a common laborer, Luis had proved an apt pupil and as the work went on had been given greater responsibility. A week after the work had started at Gavarnie, he had shown up again.

'I heard you were here,' he'd said. 'What do you have for me?'

As he came around a sharp bend in the trail, Boyd saw him, sitting cross-legged in front of the weather-beaten tent, holding the primitive pipe of his to his lips, piping away.

That was exactly what it was – piping. Whatever music came out of the pipe was primitive and elemental. Scarcely music, although Boyd would admit that he knew nothing about music. Four notes – would it be four notes? he wondered. A hollow bone with an elongated slot as a mouthpiece, two drilled holes for stops.

Once he had asked Luis about it. 'I've never seen anything like it,' he had said. Luis had told him, 'You don't see many of them. In remote villages here and there, hidden away in the mountains.'

Boyd left the path and walked across the grassy terrace, sat down beside Luis, who took down the pipe and laid it in his lap.

'I thought you were gone,' Luis said. 'The others left a couple of days ago.'

'Back for one last look,' said Boyd.

'You are reluctant to leave it?'

'Yes, I suppose I am.'

Below them the valley spread out in autumn browns and tans, the small river a silver ribbon in the sunlight, the red roofs of the village a splash of color beside the river.

'It's nice up here,' said Boyd. 'Time and time again, I catch myself trying to imagine what it might have been like at the time the paintings were done. Not much different than it is now, perhaps. The mountains would be unchanged. There'd have been no fields in the valley, but it probably would have been natural pasture. A few trees here and there, but not too many of them. Good hunting. There'd have been grass for the grazing animals. I have even tried to figure out where the people would've camped. My guess would be where the village is now.'

He looked around at Luis. The man still sat upon the grass, the pipe resting in his lap. He was smiling quietly, as if he might be smiling to himself. The small black beret sat squarely on his head, his tanned face was round and smooth, the black hair close-clipped, the blue shirt open at the throat. A young man, strong, not a wrinkle on his face.

'You love your work,' said Luis.

'I'm devoted to it. So are you, Luis,' Boyd said.

'It's not my work.'

'Your work or not,' said Boyd, 'you do it well. Would you like to go with me? One last look around.'

'I need to run an errand in the village.'

'I thought I'd find you gone,' said Boyd. 'I was surprised to hear your pipe.'

'I'll go soon,' said Luis. 'Another day or two. No reason to stay but, like you, I like this place. I have no place to go, no one needing me. Nothing's lost by staying a few more days.'

'As long as you like,' said Boyd. 'The place is yours. Before too long, the government will be setting up a caretaker arrangement, but the government moves with due deliberation.'

'Then I may not see you again,' said Luis.

'I took a couple of days to drive to Roncesvalles,' said Boyd. 'That's the place where the Gascons slaughtered Charlemagne's rearguard in 778.'

'I've heard of the place,' said Luis.

'I'd always wanted to see it. Never had the time. The Charlemagne chapel is in ruins, but I am told masses are still said in the village chapel for the dead paladins. When I returned from the trip, I couldn't resist the urge to see the cave again.'

'I am glad of that,' said Luis. 'May I be impertinent?'

'You're never impertinent,' said Boyd.

'Before you go, could we break bread once more together? Tonight, perhaps, I'll prepare an omelet.'

Boyd hesitated, gagging down a suggestion that Luis dine with him. Then he said, 'I'd be delighted, Luis. I'll bring a bottle of good wine.'

2

Holding the flashlight centered on the rock wall, Boyd bent to examine the rock more closely. He had not imagined it; he had been right. Here, in this particular spot, the rock was not solid. It was broken into several pieces, but with the several pieces flush with the rest of the wall. Only by chance could the break have been spotted. Had he not been looking directly at it, watching for it as he swept the light across the wall, he would have missed it. It was strange, he thought, that someone else, during the time they had been working in the cave, had not found it. There'd not been much that they'd missed.

He held his breath, feeling a little foolish at the holding of it, for, after all, it might mean nothing. Frost cracks, perhaps, although he knew that he was wrong. It would be unusual to find frost cracks here.

He took the hammer out of his belt and, holding the flashlight in one hand, trained on the spot, he forced the chisel end of the hammer into one of the cracks. The edge went in easily. He pried gently and the crack widened. Under more pressure, the piece of rock moved out. He laid down the hammer and flash, seized the slab of rock and pulled it free. Beneath it were two other slabs and they both came free as easily as the first. There were others as well and he also took them out. Kneeling on the floor of the cave, he directed the light into the fissure that he had uncovered.

Big enough for a man to crawl into, but at the prospect he remained for the moment undecided. Alone, he'd be taking a chance to do it. If something happened, if he should get stuck, if a fragment of rock should shift and pin him or fall upon him, there'd be no rescue. Or probably no rescue in time to save him. Luis would come back to the camp and wait for him, but should he fail to make an appearance, Luis more than likely would take it as a rebuke for impertinence or an American's callous disregard of him. It would never occur to him that Boyd might be trapped in the cave.

Still, it was his last chance. Tomorrow he'd have to drive to Paris to catch his plane. And this whole thing was intriguing; it was not something to be ignored. The fissure must have some significance; otherwise, why should it have been walled up so carefully? Who, he wondered, would have walled it up? No one, certainly, in recent times. Anyone, finding the hidden entrance to the cave, almost immediately would have seen the paintings and would have spread the word. So the entrance to the fissure must have been blocked by one who would have been unfamiliar with the significance of the paintings or by one to whom they could have been commonplace.

It was something, he decided, that could not be passed up; he would have to go in. He secured the hammer to his belt, picked up the flashlight and began to crawl.

The fissure ran straight and easy for a hundred feet or more. It offered barely room enough for crawling, but other than that, no great difficulties. Then, without warning, it came to an end. Boyd lay in it, directing the flash beam ahead of him, staring in consternation at the smooth wall of rock that came down to cut the fissure off.

It made no sense. Why should someone go to the trouble of walling off an empty fissure? He could have missed something on the way, but thinking of it, he was fairly sure he hadn't. His progress had been slow and he had kept the flash directed ahead of him every inch of the way. Certainly if there had been anything out of the ordinary, he would have seen it.

Then a thought came to him and slowly, with some effort, he began to turn himself around, so that his back rather than his front, lay on the fissure floor. Directing the beam upward, he had his answer. In the roof of the fissure gaped a hole.

Cautiously, he raised himself into a sitting position. Reaching up, he found handholds on the projecting rock and pulled himself erect. Swinging the flash around, he saw that the hole opened, not into another fissure, but into a bubblelike cavity – small, no more than six feet in any dimension. The walls and ceiling of the cavity were smooth, as if a bubble of plastic rock had existed here for a moment at some time in the distant geologic past when the mountains had been heaving upward leaving behind it as it drained away a bubble forever frozen into smooth and solid stone.

As he swung the flash across the bubble, he gasped in astonishment. Colorful animals capered around the entire expanse of stone. Bison played leapfrog. Horses cantered in a chorus line. Mammoths turned somersaults. All around the bottom perimeter, just above the floor, dancing deer, standing on their hind legs, joined hands and jigged, antlers swaying gracefully.

'For the love of Christ!' said Boyd.

Here was Stone Age Disney.

If it was the Stone Age. Could some jokester have crawled into the area in fairly recent times to paint the animals in this grotto? Thinking it over, he rejected the idea. So far as he had been able to ascertain, no one in the valley, nor in the entire region, for that matter, had known of the cave until a shepherd had found it several years before when a lamb had blundered into it. The entrance was small and apparently for centuries had been masked by a heavy growth of brush and bracken.

Too, the execution of the paintings had a prehistoric touch to them. Perspective played but a small part. The paintings had that curious flat look that distinguished most prehistoric art. There was no background – no

horizon line, no trees, no grass or flowers, no clouds, no
sense of sky. Although, he reminded himself, anyone who
had any knowledge of cave painting probably would
have been aware of all these factors and worked to
duplicate them.

Yet, despite the noncharacteristic antics of the painted
animals, the pictures did have the feeling of cave art.
What ancient man, Boyd asked himself, what kind of
ancient man, would have painted gamboling bison and
tumbling mammoths? While the situation did not hold in
all cave art, all the paintings in this particular cave were
deadly serious – conservative as to form and with a
forthright, honest attempt to portray the animals as the
artists had seen them. There was no frivolity, not even
the imprint of paint-smeared human hands as so often
happened in other caves. The men who had worked in
this cave had not as yet been corrupted by the symbolism
that had crept in, apparently rather late in the prehistoric painting cycle.

So who had been this clown who had crept off by
himself in this hidden cavern to paint his comic animals?
That he had been an accomplished painter there could
be no doubt. This artist's techniques and executions
were without flaw.

Boyd hauled himself up through the hole, slid out onto
the two-foot ledge that ran all around the hole,
crouching, for there was no room to stand. Much of the
painting, he realised, must have been done with the artist
lying flat upon his back, reaching up to the work on the
curving ceiling.

He swept the beam of the flashlight along the ledge.
Halfway around, he halted the light and jiggled it back
and forth to focus upon something that was placed upon
the ledge, something that undoubtedly had been left by
the artist when he had finished his work and gone away.

Leaning forward, Boyd squinted to make out what it

was. It looked like the shoulder blade of a deer; beside the shoulder blade lay a lump of stone.

Cautiously, he edged his way around the ledge. He had been right. It was the shoulder blade of a deer. Upon the flat surface of it lay a lumpy substance. Paint? he wondered, the mixture of animal fat and mineral earths the prehistoric artists used a paints? He focused the flash closer and there was no doubt. It was paint, spread over the surface of the bone which had served as a palette, with some of the paint lying in thicker lumps ready for use, but never used, paint dried and mummified and bearing imprints of some sort. He leaned close, bringing his face down to within a few inches of the paint, shining the light upon the surface. The imprints, he saw, were fingerprints, some of them sunk deep – the signature of that ancient, long-dead man who had worked here, crouching even as Boyd now crouched, shoulders hunched against the curving stone. He put out his hand to touch the palette, then pulled it back. Symbolic, yes, this move to touch, this reaching out to touch the man who painted – but symbolic only; a gesture with too many centuries between.

He shifted the flashlight beam to the small block of stone that lay beside the shoulder blade. A lamp – hollowed out sandstone, a hollow to hold the fat and the chunk of moss that served as a wick. The fat and wick were long since gone, but a thin film of soot still remained around the rim of the hollow that had held them.

Finishing his work, the artist had left his tools behind him, had even left the lamp, perhaps still guttering, with the fat almost finished – had left it here and let himself down into the fissure, crawling it in darkness. To him, perhaps, there was no need of light. He could crawl the tunnel by touch and familiarity. He must have crawled the route many times, for the work upon these walls had taken long, perhaps many days.

So he had left, crawling through the fissure, using the blocks of stone to close the opening to the fissure, then had walked away, scrambling down the slope to the valley where grazing herds had lifted their heads to watch him, then had gone back to grazing.

But when has this all happened? Probably, Boyd told himself, after the cave itself had been painted, perhaps even after the paintings in the cave had lost much of whatever significance they originally would have held – one lone man coming back to paint his secret animals in his secret place. Painting them as a mockery of the pompous, magical importance of the main cave paintings? Or as a protest against the stuffy conservatism of the original paintings? Or simply as a bubbling chuckle, an exuberance of life, perhaps even a joyous rebellion against the grimness and the simple-mindedness of the hunting magic? A rebel, he thought, a prehistoric rebel – an intellectual rebel? Or, perhaps, simply a man with a viewpoint slightly skewed from the philosophy of his time?

But this was that other man, that ancient man. Now how about himself? Having found the grotto, what did he do next? What would be the best way to handle it? Certainly he could not turn his back upon it and walk away, as the artist, leaving his palette and his lamp behind him, had walked away. For this was an important discovery. There could be no question of that. Here was a new and unsuspected approach to the prehistoric mind, a facet of ancient thinking that never had been guessed.

Leave everything as it lay, close up the fissure and make a phone call to Washington and another one to Paris, unpack his bags and settle down for a few more weeks of work. Get back the photographers and other members of the crew – do a job of it. Yes, he told himself, that was the way to do it.

Something lying behind the lamp, almost hidden by the sandstone lamp, glinted in the light. Something white and small.

Still crouched over, Boyd shuffled forward to get a better look.

It was a piece of bone, probably a leg bone from a small grazing animal. He reached out and picked it up and, having seen what it was, hunched unmoving over it, not quite sure what to make of it.

It was a pipe, a brother to the pipe that Luis carried in his jacket pocket, had carried in his pocket since that first day he'd met him, years ago. There was the mouthpiece slot, there the two round stops. In that long-gone day when the paintings had been done the artist had hunched here, in the flickering of the lamp, and had played softly to himself, those simple piping airs that Luis had played almost every evening, after work was done.

'Merciful Jesus,' Boyd said, almost prayerfully, 'it simply cannot be!'

He stayed there, frozen in his crouch, the thoughts hammering in his mind while he tried to push the thoughts away. They would not go away. He'd drive them away for just a little distance, then they'd come surging back to overwhelm him.

Finally, grimly, he broke the trance in which the thoughts had held him. He worked deliberately, forcing himself to do what he knew must be done.

He took off his windbreaker and carefully wrapped the shoulder blade palette and the pipe inside, leaving the lamp. He let himself down into the fissure and crawled, carefully protecting the bundle that he carried. In the cave again, he meticulously fitted the blocks of stone together to block the fissure mouth, scraped together handfuls of soil from the cave floor and smeared it on the face of the blocks, wiping it away, but leaving a small clinging film to mask the opening to all but the most inquiring eye.

Luis was not at his camp on the terrace below the cave mouth; he was still on his errand into the village.

When he reached his hotel, Boyd made his telephone call to Washington. He skipped the call to Paris.

3

The last leaves of October were blowing in the autumn wind and a weak sun, not entirely obscured by the floating clouds, shone down on Washington.

John Roberts was waiting for him on the park bench. They nodded at one another, without speaking, and Boyd sat down beside his friend.

'You took a big chance,' said Roberts. 'What would have happened if the customs people . . .'

'I wasn't too worried,' Boyd said. 'I knew this man in Paris. For years he's been smuggling stuff into America. He's good at it and he owed me one. What have you got?'

'Maybe more than you want to hear.'

'Try me.'

'The fingerprints match,' said Roberts.

'You were able to get a reading on the paint impressions?'

'Loud and clear.'

'The FBI?'

'Yes, the FBI. It wasn't easy, but I have a friend or two.'

'And the dating?'

'No problem. The bad part of the job was convincing my man this was top secret. He's still not sure it is.'

'Will he keep his mouth shut?'

'I think so. Without evidence no one would believe him. It would sound like a fairy story.'

'Tell me.'

'Twenty-two thousand. Plus or minus three hundred years.'

'And the prints do match. The bottle prints and . . .'

'I told you they match. Now will you tell me how in he'l a man who lived twenty-two thousand years ago could leave his prints on a wine bottle that was manufactured last year.'

'It's a long story,' said Boyd. 'I don't know if I should. First, where do you have the shoulder blade?'

'Hidden,' said Roberts. 'Well hidden. You can have it back, and the bottle, any time you wish.'

Boyd shrugged. 'Not yet. Not for a while. Perhaps never.'

'Never?'

'Look, John, I have to think it out.'

'What a hell of a mess,' said Roberts. 'No one wants the stuff. No one would dare to have it. Smithsonian wouldn't touch it with a ten-foot pole. I haven't asked. They don't even know about it. But I know they wouldn't want it. There's something isn't there, about sneaking artifacts out of a country . . .'

'Yes, there is,' said Boyd.

'And now you don't want it.'

'I didn't say that. I just said let it stay where it is for a time. It's safe, isn't it?'

'It's safe. And now . . .'

'I told you it is a long story. I'll try to make it short. There's this man – a Basque. He came to me ten years ago when I was doing the rock shelter . . .'

Roberts nodded. 'I remember that one.'

'He wanted work and I gave him work. He broke in fast, caught onto the techniques immediately. Became a valuable man. That often happens with native laborers. They seem to have the feel for their own antiquity. And then when we started work on the cave he showed up again. I was glad to see him. The two of us, as a matter of fact, are fairly good friends. On my last night at the cave he cooked a marvelous omelet – eggs, tomato, green

pimentoes, onions, sausages and home-cured ham. I
brought a bottle of wine.'

'*The* bottle?'

'Yes, *the* bottle.'

'So go ahead.'

'He played a pipe. A bone pipe. A squeaky sort of
thing. Not too much music in it . . .'

'There was a pipe . . .'

'Not that pipe. Another pipe. The same kind of pipe,
but not the one our man has. Two pipes the same. One in
a living man's pocket, the other beside the shoulder
blade. There were things about this man I'm telling you
of. Nothing that hit you between the eyes. Just little
things. You would notice something and then, some time
later, maybe quite a bit later, there'd be something else,
but by the time that happened, you'd have forgotten the
first incident and not tie the two together. Mostly it was
that he knew too much. Little things a man like him
would not be expected to know. Even things that no one
knew. Bits and pieces of knowledge that slipped out of
him, maybe without his realising it. And his eyes. I
didn't realise that until later, not until I'd found the
second pipe and began to think about the other things.
But I was talking about his eyes. In appearance he is a
young man, a never-aging man, but his eyes are old . . .'

'Tom, you said he is a Basque.'

'That's right.'

'Isn't there some belief that the Basques may have
descended from the Cro-Magnons?'

'There is such a theory. I have thought of it.'

'Could this man of yours be a Cro-Magnon?'

'I'm beginning to think he is.'

'But think of it – twenty thousand years!'

'Yes, I know,' said Boyd.

4

Boyd heard the piping when he reached the bottom of the trail that led up to the cave. The notes were ragged, torn by the wind. The Pyrenees stood up against the high blue sky.

Tucking the bottle of wine more securely underneath his arm, Boyd began the climb. Below him lay the redness of the village rooftops and the sere brown of autumn that spread across the valley. The piping continued, lifting and falling as the wind tugged at it playfully.

Luis sat cross-legged in front of the tattered tent. When he saw Boyd, he put the pipe in his lap and sat waiting.

Boyd sat down beside him, handing him the bottle. Luis took it and began working on the cork.

'I heard you were back,' he said. 'How went the trip?'

'It went well,' said Boyd.

'So now you know,' said Luis.

Boyd nodded. 'I think you wanted me to know. Why should you have wanted that?'

'The years grow long,' said Luis. 'The burden heavy. It is lonely, all alone.'

'You are not alone.'

'It's lonely when no one knows you. You now are the first who has really known me.'

'But the knowing will be short. A few years more and again no one will know you.'

'This lifts the burden for a time,' said Luis. 'Once you are gone, I will be able to take it up again. And there is something . . .'

'Yes, what is it, Luis?'

'You say when you are gone there'll be no one again. Does that mean . . .'

'If what you're getting at is whether I will spread the word, no, I won't. Not unless you wish it. I have thought on what would happen to you if the world were told.'

'I have certain defenses. You can't live as long as I have if you fail in your defenses.'

'What kind of defenses?'

'Defenses. That is all.'

'I'm sorry if I pried. There's one other thing. If you wanted me to know, you took a long chance. Why, if something had gone wrong, if I had failed to find the grotto . . .'

'I had hoped, at first, that the grotto would not be necessary. I had thought you might have guessed, on your own.'

'I knew there was something wrong. But this is so outrageous I couldn't have trusted myself even had I guessed. You know it's outrageous, Luis. And if I'd not found the grotto . . . Its finding was pure chance, you know.'

'If you hadn't, I would have waited. Some other time, some other year, there would have been someone else. Some other way to betray myself.'

'You could have told me.'

'Cold, you mean?'

'That's what I mean. I would not have believed you, of course. Not at first.'

'Don't you understand? I could not have told you. The concealment now is second nature. One of the defenses I talked about. I simply could not have brought myself to tell you, or anyone.'

'Why me? Why wait all these years until I came along?'

'I did not wait, Boyd. There were others, at different times. None of them worked out. I had to find, you must understand, someone who had the strength to face it. Not one who would run screaming madly. I knew you would not run screaming.'

'I've had time to think it through,' Boyd said. 'I've come to terms with it. I can accept the fact, but not too well, only barely. Luis, do you have some explanation? How come you are so different from the rest of us?'

'No idea at all. No inkling. At one time, I thought there must be others like me and I sought for them. I found none. I no longer seek.'

The cork came free and he handed the bottle of wine to Boyd. 'You go first,' he said steadily.

Boyd lifted the bottle and drank. He handed it to Luis. He watched him as he drank. Wondering, as he watched, how he could be sitting here, talking calmly with a man who had lived, who had stayed young through twenty thousand years. His gorge rose once again against acceptance of the fact – but it had to be a fact. The shoulder blade, the small amount of organic matter still remaining in the pigment, had measured out to twenty-two thousand years. There was no question that the prints in the paint had matched the prints upon the bottle. He had raised one question back in Washington, hoping there might be evidence of hoax. Would it have been possible, he had asked, that the ancient pigment, the paint used by the prehistoric artist, could have been reconstituted, the fingerprints impressed upon it, and then replaced in the grotto? Impossible was the answer. Any reconstitution of the pigment, had it been possible, would have shown up in the analysis. There had been nothing of the sort – the pigment dated to twenty thousand years ago. There was no question of that.

'All right, Cro-Magnon,' said Boyd, 'tell me how you did it. How does a man survive as long as you have? You do not age, of course. Your body will not accept disease. But I take it you are not immune to violence or to accident. You've lived in a violent world. How does a man sidestep accident and violence for two hundred centuries?'

'There were times early,' Luis said, 'when I came close to not surviving. For a long time, I did not realise the kind of thing I was. Sure, I lived longer, stayed younger than all the others – I would guess, however, that I didn't begin to notice this until I began to realise that all the people I had known in my early life were dead – dead for a long, long time. I knew then that I was different from the rest. About the same time others began to notice I was different. They became suspicious of me. Some of them resented me. Others thought I was some sort of evil spirit. Finally I had to flee the tribe. I became a skulking outcast. That was when I began to learn the principles of survival.'

'And those principles?'

'You keep a low profile. You don't stand out. You attract no attention to yourself. You cultivate a cowardly attitude. You are never brave. You take no risks. You let others do the dirty work. You never volunteer. You skulk and run and hide. You grow a skin that's thick; you don't give a damn what others think of you. You shed all your noble attributes, your social consciousness. You shuck your loyalty to tribe or folk or country. You're not a patriot. You live for yourself alone. You're an observer, never a participant. You scuttle around the edges of things. And you become so self-centered that you come to believe that no blame should attach to you, that you are living in the only logical way a man can live. You went to Roncesvalles the other day, remember?'

'Yes. I mentioned I'd been there. You said you'd heard of it.'

'Heard of it. Hell, I was there the day it happened – August 15th, 778. An observer, not a participant. A cowardly little bastard who tagged along behind the noble band of Gascons who did in Charlemagne. Gascons, hell. That's the fancy name for them. They were Basques, pure and simple. The meanest crew of men who ever drew the breath of life. Some Basques may be noble, but not this band. Not the kind of warriors who'd stand up face to face with the Franks. They hid up in the pass and rolled rocks down on all those puissant knights. But it wasn't the knights who held their interest. It was the wagon train. They weren't out to fight a war or to avenge a wrong. They were out for loot. Although little good it did them.'

'Why do you say that?'

'It was this way,' said Luis. 'They knew the rest of the Frankish army would return when the rearguard didn't come up and they had not the stomach for that. They stripped the dead knights of their golden spurs, their armor and fancy clothes, the money bags they carried and loaded all of it on the wagons and got out of there. A few miles further on, deep in the mountains, they holed up and hid. In a deep canyon where they thought they would be safe. But if they should be found, they had what amounted to a fort. A half mile or so below the place they camped, the canyon narrowed and twisted sharply. A lot of boulders had fallen down at that point, forming a barricade that could have been held by a handful of men against any assault that could be launched against it. By this time, I was a long way off. I smelled something wrong, I knew something most unpleasant was about to happen. That's another thing about this survival business. You develop special senses. You get so you can smell out trouble, well ahead of time. I heard what happened later.'

He lifted the bottle and had another drink. He handed it to Boyd.

'Don't leave me hanging,' said Boyd. 'Tell me what did happen.'

'In the night,' said Luis, 'a storm came up. One of those sudden, brutal summer thunderstorms. This time it was a cloudburst. My brave fellow Gascons died to the man. That's the price of bravery.'

Boyd took a drink, lowered the bottle, held it to his chest, cuddling it.

'You know about this,' he said. 'No one else does. Perhaps no one had ever wondered what happened to those Gascons who gave Charlemagne the bloody nose. You must know of other things. Christ, man, you've lived history. You didn't stick to this area.'

'No. At times I wandered. I had an itching foot. There were things to see. I had to keep moving along. I couldn't stay in one place any length of time or it would be noticed that I wasn't aging.'

'You lived through the Black Death,' said Boyd. 'You watched the Roman legions. You heard first hand of Attila. You skulked along on Crusades. You walked the streets of ancient Athens.'

'Not Athens,' said Luis. 'Somehow Athens was never to my taste. I spent some time in Sparta. Sparta, I tell you – that was really something.'

'You're an educated man,' said Boyd. 'Where did you go to school?'

'Paris, for a time, in the fourteenth century. Later on at Oxford. After that at other places. Under different names. Don't try tracing me through the schools that I attended.'

'You could write a book,' said Boyd. 'It would set new sales records. You'd be a millionaire. One book and you'd be a millionaire.'

'I can't afford to be a millionaire. I can't be noticed and millionaires are noticed. I'm not in want. I've never been in want. There's always treasure for a skulker to pick up. I have caches here and there. I get along all right.'

Luis was right, Boyd told himself. He couldn't be a millionaire. He couldn't write a book. In no way could he be famous, stand out in any way. In all things, he must remain unremarkable, always anonymous.

The principles of survival, he had said. And this part of it, although not all of it. He had mentioned the art of smelling trouble, the hunch ability. There would be, as well, the wisdom, the street savvy, the cynicism that a man would pick up along the way, the expertise, the ability to judge character, an insight into human reaction, some knowledge concerning the use of power, power of every sort, economic power, political power, religious power.

Was the man still human, he wondered, or had he, in twenty thousand years, become something more than human? Had he advanced that one vital step that would place him beyond humankind, the king of being that would come after man?

'One thing more,' said Boyd. 'Why the Disney paintings?'

'They were painted some time later than the others,' Luis told him. 'I painted some of the earlier stuff in the cave. The fishing bear is mine. I knew about the grotto. I found it and said nothing. No reason I should have kept it secret. Just one of those little items one hugs to himself to make himself important. I know something you don't know – silly stuff like that. Later I came back to paint the grotto. The cave art was so deadly serious. Such terribly silly magic. I told myself painting should be fun. So I came back, after the tribe had moved and painted simply for the fun of it. How did it strike you, Boyd?'

'Damn good art,' said Boyd.

'I was afraid you wouldn't find the grotto and I couldn't help you. I knew you had seen the cracks in the wall; I watched you one day looking at them. I counted on your remembering them. And I counted on you seeing the fingerprints and finding the pipe. All pure serendipity, of course. I had nothing in mind when I left the paint with the fingerprints and the pipe. The pipe, of course, was the tip-off and I was confident you'd at least be curious. But I couldn't be sure. When we ate that night, here by the campfire, you didn't mention the grotto and I was afraid you'd blew it. But when you made off with the bottle, sneaking it away, I knew I had it made. And now the big question. Will you let the world in on the grotto paintings?'

'I don't know. I'll have to think about it. What are your thoughts on the matter?'

'I'd just as soon you didn't.'

'Okay,' said Boyd. 'Not for the time at least. Is there anything else I can do for you? Anything you want?'

'You've done the best thing possible,' said Luis. 'You know who I am, what I am. I don't know why that's so important to me, but it is. A matter of identity, I suppose. When you die, which I hope will be a long time from now, then, once again, there'll be no one who knows. But the knowledge that one man did know, and what is more important, understood, will sustain me through the centuries. A minute – I have something for you.'

He rose and went into the tent, came back with a sheet of paper, handing it to Boyd. It was a topographical survey of some sort.

'I've put a cross on it,' said Luis. 'To mark the spot.'

'What spot?'

'Where you'll find the Charlemagne treasure of Roncesvalles. The wagons and the treasure would have been carried down the canyon in the flood. The turn in the canyon and the boulder barricade I spoke of would have blocked them. You'll find them there, probably under a deep layer of gravel and debris.'

Boyd looked up questioningly from the map.

'It's worth going after,' said Luis. 'Also it provides another check against the validity of my story.'

'I believe you,' said Boyd. 'I need no further evidence.'

'Ah, well!' said Luis, 'it wouldn't hurt. And now, it's time to go.'

'Time to go! We have a lot to talk about.'

'Later, perhaps,' said Luis. 'We'll bump into one another time to time. I'll make a point we do. But now it's time to go.'

He started down the path and Boyd sat watching him.

After a few steps, Luis halted and half-turned back to Boyd.

'It seems to me,' he said in explanation, 'it's always time to go.'

Boyd stood and watched him move down the trail toward the village. There was about the moving figure a deep sense of loneliness – the most lonely man in all the world.

Science Fiction and Fantasy from Methuen Paperbacks

While every effort is made to keep prices low, it is sometimes necessary to increase prices at short notice. Methuen Paperbacks reserves the right to show new retail prices on covers which may differ from those previously advertised in the text or elsewhere.

The prices shown below were correct at the time of going to press.

☐	413 55450 3	**Half-Past Human**	T J Bass	£1.95
☐	413 58160 8	**Rod of Light**	Barrington J Bayley	£2.50
☐	417 04130 6	**Colony**	Ben Bova	£2.50
☐	413 57910 7	**Orion**	Ben Bova	£2.95
☐	417 07280 5	**Voyagers**	Ben Bova	£1.95
☐	417 06760 7	**Hawk of May**	Gillian Bradshaw	£1.95
☐	413 56290 5	**Chronicles of Morgaine**	C J Cherryh	£2.95
☐	413 51310 6	**Downbelow Station**	C J Cherryh	£1.95
☐	413 51350 5	**Little Big**	John Crowley	£3.95
☐	417 06200 1	**The Golden Man**	Philip K Dick	£1.75
☐	417 02590 4	**The Man Who Japed**	Philip K Dick	£1.75
☐	413 58860 2	**Wasp**	Eric Frank Russell	£2.50
☐	413 59770 9	**The Alchemical Marriage of Alistair Crompton**	Robert Sheckley	£2.25
☐	413 59990 6	**All Flesh is Grass**	Clifford D Simak	£2.50
☐	413 58800 9	**A Heritage of Stars**	Clifford D Simak	£2.50
☐	413 55590 9	**The Werewolf Principle**	Clifford D Simak	£1.95
☐	413 58640 5	**Where the Evil Dwells**	Clifford D Simak	£2.50
☐	413 52000 5	**The Buccaneers of Lan-Kern**	Peter Tremayne	£1.95
☐	413 54600 4	**Raven of Destiny**	Peter Tremayne	£1.95
☐	413 56840 7	**This Immortal**	Roger Zelazny	£1.95
☐	413 56850 4	**The Dream Master**	Roger Zelazny	£1.95

All these books are available at your bookshop or newsagent, or can be ordered direct from the publisher. Just tick the titles you want and fill in the form below.

Methuen Paperbacks, Cash Sales Department,
PO Box 11, Falmouth,
Cornwall TR10 109EN.

Please send cheque or postal order, no currency, for purchase price quoted and allow the following for postage and packing:

UK	55p for the first book, 22p for the second book and 14p for each additional book ordered to a maximum charge of £1.75.
BFPO and Eire	55p for the first book, 22p for the second book and 14p for each next seven books, thereafter 8p per book.
Overseas Customers	£1.00 for the first book plus 25p per copy for each additional book.

NAME (Block Letters) ....

ADDRESS..

....